A
Harlequin
Romance

OTHER
Harlequin Romances
by JANE ARBOR

Many of these titles are available at your local bookseller, or through the Harlequin Reader Service.

For a free catalogue listing all available Harlequin Romances, send your name and address to:

HARLEQUIN READER SERVICE,
M.P.O. Box 707, Niagara Falls, N.Y. 14302
Canadian address: Stratford, Ontario, Canada.

or use order coupon at back of book.

THE FLOWER ON THE ROCK

by

JANE ARBOR

HARLEQUIN BOOKS

TORONTO
WINNIPEG

Original hard cover edition published in 1972
by Mills & Boon Limited, 17-19 Foley Street,
London W1A 1DR, England

© Jane Arbor 1972

SBN 373-01665-4

Harlequin edition published March 1973

Printed in Canada

The quotation from 'Odysseus Dying' by
Sheila Wingfield is by permission of
Barrie & Jenkins Ltd.

CHAPTER I

ABOVE, a midday sky whose fierce glare was diminished by the greater glare of the sun. Below, a rolling foam of cloud which from time to time sent cotton-wool wisps to drift and disappear, heat-dissolved, in the path of the aircraft. Far below again, the boundless stretch of the South Pacific, not to be glimpsed until flying height began to be lost in readiness for the touchdown on the island of Grand'terre, journey's end.

The aircraft cabin was cool, quiet, its mere half-complement of passengers free to choose or change their seating as they pleased.

Honor, travelling first-class by air at her employers' expense for the first time in her life, had a rank of three seats to herself; her nearest neighbour was the man across the gangway who was making notes from papers he had taken from his briefcase soon after the take-off warning signal had winked out.

Honor's mild interest studied him. She couldn't quite place him. Tycoon luggage. (He had stood abreast with her at the weighing-desk at Sydney Airport.) Light tropical suiting, his silk polo-neck shirt informal. All those papers – the executive type perhaps? N-no, or at least not wholly, she decided. For though in this climate every office-wallah was as bronzed as the next man, there was some indefinably extra touch of the outdoors to this one.

Those strong broad hands weren't the everyday

slaves of a fountain pen for sure. The tawny eyes which went with the darker tawny hair were used to looking farther afield than the confines of an office. There was something patrician about that high-boned nose. . . . He commanded men . . . and land and – But there Honor checked with a small laugh at herself which brought her companion's glance briefly to her and away again. Just how fanciful could one get about strangers who happened to catch one's interest for the passage of a journey! Yet in the case of the man opposite she would have liked to know how true her speculation was.

When he rose and went back towards the galley she heard him ask for cigars and remain chatting to the steward. She herself idly fingered the papers she had brought aboard with her, selecting one in which she had begun the crossword puzzle while waiting for the flight to be called. Absorbed, her pencil poised, she was aware of his return only when he paused by her seat, his hand on its high back. She looked up, met the appraisal of his eyes before he nodded at the paper in her hand.

"Stumped?" he asked.

She smiled. "For the moment, yes," she said.

"What over?"

"This clue. It's a quotation. By the reference, 'Circe' ought to fit. But it's only five letters and the clue needs seven."

"May I see? Perhaps I can help?" Without waiting for permission, he slid his long legs beneath the table and sat beside her. "Where?" he asked.

"This one –" Her pencil pointed and his hand upon

hers lingered for a moment as he took the paper from her to read aloud,

" 'I think Odysseus, as he dies, forgets

" 'Which was' – blank, 'which Penelope . . .' ' "

He turned to look at her with a half smile. "You get the reference, then?"

"Don't I? Doesn't it mean Circe, the island nymph who kept Odysseus idling at her side for seven years while his wife Penelope remained faithful to him at home?"

"Exactly. Vamp versus Virtue, then as now."

"But Penelope won in the end. Odysseus went back to her. He had only been dallying with Circe."

"It takes two to dally. Circe must have laid on enough charm to keep him all that time. However, full marks for your Greek mythology, though as you say, Circe doesn't fit the clue."

Honor pondered, "No –"

"Then why not try 'Calypso'? You already have the 'C' in place."

"Calypso? Oh yes – another name for Circe, of course! Thank you so much!"

"You're welcome," her companion said, mimicking an American accent not his own, which was not wholly Southern Hemisphere either, Honor thought. As she filled in the clue she was prepared for him to move away, though when he stayed to ask what was the next clue, she was glad, telling herself that it was always more fun to tackle crossword puzzles in duet, rather than alone.

Between them they finished the puzzle. Then he half-turned in his seat to face her. "Are you going on holiday to Grand'terre?" he asked casually.

"No, to a job," she told him, and when he seemed to expect her to enlarge on that, she added, "I'm going to the Grand'terre plant of Universal Nickel Holdings. They sponsor medical services for their staffs and their workers and the workers' dependants at their plants all over the world. I'm to be medical secretary to their Grand'terre doctor, Dr. Adam Page."

He nodded recognition of the name. So he must know Grand'terre, perhaps live there, she thought, as he went on, "You've met Page, perhaps? You know the island already?"

Honor didn't and hadn't met her colleague-to-be. "In fact –" she began, before deciding that the unwelcome haste of her appointment to Grand'terre was of no interest to this stranger. Instead she asked whether he himself lived on the island.

"A few kilometres out from the city, Port Maré, on the west coast," adding that a cousin of his had also recently taken a post with Nickel Holdings, before he queried Honor's accent.

"You are not Australian born? English, I'd say?"

She confirmed, "Yes, though I've been in Sydney since my parents emigrated there, ten years ago. They decided to go back last year. But I had a job – not with Nickel Holdings then – and I wanted to stay on."

"And you were free to make your own choice?"

She knew she had flushed at his calculating gaze. "Oh, you mean –? Yes, I was twenty, and my people didn't mind."

"And now you are moving to Grand'terre? Fresh woods – h'm? Well, enjoy our island, won't you? It's

10

pleasant enough, though the climate has its ugly moments. It is French-governed, as you'll know. Social clubs galore, from night to yacht . . . bars, dancings, French boutiques, flora in full technicolor, beaches, coral reef and out-islands all laid on. Nickel Holdings' smelting chimneys on the tropic skyline its one blemish; as it were, our hairshirt. But when a tropical terrain throws up mineral ores as England boasts coal, who can blame the nickel men for muscling in? Anyway, I'll wish you fun between your medical chores, and I'd say" – his eye measured her in male approval – "you'll find the opportunities are rife!" With which he eased himself out from his seat beside her and returned to his own and to his paperwork.

He had wished her "fun". Ironic that, when she would not have been going to his home island at all, had she been allowed to refuse, Honor thought. For Grand'terre had associations which, though time was blunting their impact, she didn't want revived. She could argue that they need not be; that she would have been foolish and blameworthy if she had passed up an interesting job in an island of the size and population of Grand'terre. But she had been tempted to shun it and might have done, had it not been for the unwritten obligations she had to her new employers. Nickel Holdings Inc., making it coldly clear it could afford little concern for its employees' personal reluctances or scruples, had given her small choice. And so, after a difficult quarter of an hour of demur, she had finally bowed to the edict which, almost at the last minute before her appointment elsewhere, had posted her instead to the plant on Grand'terre.

11

Staring out at the nothingness of the foam-pillow of cloud below and the stark sky above, Honor thought back to the brief eruption of charm and romantic drive which Piers Sabre had been in her life.

He had happened to her at the time of her loneliest reactions to her parents' departure for England. He and she had met when he was staying in Sydney, on two months' vacation from his family's plantations of copra and coffee on Grand'terre. After their initial meeting at a party, he had begun to demand all her leisure, and at the time, a little adrift and with no home ties, except those she owed her flatmate, she had willingly been monopolised by him; thrilling to the sound of his voice whenever the telephone rang for her and he was on the line, not needing to doubt that if it didn't ring tonight, then it surely would tomorrow, and if not then, some time very soon . . .

They went to the beach, to discotheques, sailing and driving. Sometimes they dined in exclusive candlelit little restaurants; sometimes they took picnic meals of seafood and a bottle of wine down to the beach; sometimes they supped on hamburgers and coffee in thick mugs from a street coffee-stall. They kissed and sometimes quarrelled and as often made it up, and ultimately came to a point where, without needing to say as much, they seemed to agree that this was no mere holiday nonsense between them; it was going to last.

The two months of Piers' vacation became three, and then, somehow, more than that. When Honor had questioned his freedom to extend it so, he had said lightly, evasively, "My sweet cabbage, what's the point of working for the family concern if it can't afford

12

one a little licence now and then?" — a reply which she had allowed to satisfy her, because she wanted him so badly to stay.

It was only later — disastrously later — that she realised how little he had told her of his background in exchange for all he had learned of hers.

Copra and coffee. To judge by his freedom with money, his share in the profits a generous one. A too-vague mention of a cousin named Arnot Lord, now the head of the family; the cousin's widowed French mother, aunt to Piers; a more detailed picture of his own twin sister, Dorice; a sketched-in description of the estate-house which had been his and Dorice's home since their parents' loss in a sailing accident while they were still children — apart from his age, approximating to her own, that was about all she had learned of his past, and for the time being, the sweet present had seemed enough. It was only at that same "later" that she was to remember with a stab of hindsight that in speaking of his twin he had said, "You would like her, darling," not "You will like her" which she could have read as a promise that she and Dorice would meet.

That was after Piers had suddenly gone, disappearing without warning, except for the scrawled note brought to Honor's flat by a stranger — a laconic farewell which told her nothing, yet said everything about his rejection of her, in no more than a dozen words. "My sweet, forget and forgive. It has to have been only a nonsense after all."

Though she concluded he had returned to Grand' terre, his home island, she had made no effort to locate him; it was all six months behind her now and the scars

13

it left had healed over. Sensibly, she cut such ties as might continue to remind her of him and lately had begun to seek another job. Her chance had come when the Australian branch of Universal Nickel Holdings had advertised for two medical secretaries and, coming straight from her secretary-receptionist post with a group of Sydney doctors, she had been appointed as one of them.

She was to be posted to a U.N.H. plant in northern New South Wales. The salary was excellent, the leave periods generous. Her contract was for two years. She would be sharing bungalow quarters with one other person. She had almost completed her final arrangements for travelling north when U.N.H. Inc. had suddenly changed its official mind.

A suitable candidate for the second vacancy had not yet been found, and as the urgency of Dr. Page on Grand'terre was the greater, Miss Troy would kindly proceed there instead.

At the news "Miss Troy" had been appalled and had shown her dismay at the switch of plan. Faintly she had argued personal reasons, her preference for the mainland of Australia, the disadvantage of her merely schoolroom French on a French-owned island. But she was met with a virtual ultimatum. Either she went where she was directed or her contract would be void. The only concession made to her was that if she could not settle down, she might apply for a transfer in six months' time. And so – what was her answer? Yes or no?

In the end, though apprehensively, she had made it yes.

The aircraft's tannoy system broke into her thoughts. "Starting descent now. As we break cloud-cover the city of Port Maré may be seen to starboard. We shall make touchdown at Touton Airport at approximately fourteen-thirty hours. Fasten your seat belts, please."

As promised, the cloud blanket parted for them a few minutes later. The sea was as blue and unruffled as the sky they left behind and then, as they circled for landing the heavy cloud allowed the sun through too, and Honor's first impressions of the coral-bound island of Grand'terre were of the dazzling white of gently curling surf, of beaches, of city buildings, and of the contrasting ochre of cliffs and the ore-bearing mountains, of the yellow of the inland savannahs, of the deep green of the rain-forests – a feast of sheer colour, though without much definition as yet.

Then the passengers were free to release themselves. Touton Airport, as characterless as every airport in the world, was a stretch of hot tarmac and the group of official buildings which was everyone's goal. Following the air hostess to the customs shed, Honor's cabin companion caught her up, deftly purloining her hand-luggage and carrying it for her.

"Touton is twenty kilometres out from the city, about the same from the U.N.H. plant. Are you to be met? By Doctor Page perhaps?" he asked.

"I don't know. I'm to share quarters with another employee of U.N.H., so she may have come for me."

"Well, if not, I'll play chauffeur, if I may. Should you get through Customs first, wait for me in the reception hall and, vice versa, I'll do the same for you."

In fact their luggage was side by side on the examination bench and they went through to the main hall together. There the tannoy crackled, then spoke – a message through even the French of which Honor recognised her own name. She halted, touched her companion on his sleeve. "That may have been for me," she said. "I've an idea I heard my name. Will it be repeated?"

"In English next –" He broke off as the mechanical voice spoke again – "A message for Miss Honor Troy at Passenger Control. Repeat – For Miss Honor Troy. Out."

"That *is* for me. I'm Honor Troy. It may be to tell me –" She broke off, appalled by the expression on her escort's face; a look which had set his mouth into hard lines, wiped every vestige of cordiality from his eyes. "Wh – what is the matter? What have I said?" she questioned the look in bewilderment.

It continued to bore down upon her, *through* her. Then he said, "Your name, of course – spoken to me. And if you don't understand, here's mine in exchange – Arnot Lord." He paused, still watching her. "You'll have heard it before, I daresay?"

She flinched, as at a blow. This, the one ill-chance which she might have been spared – that at the very outset she should meet one of Piers Sabre's family; find him at first friendly and helpful and now – what? She forced calm into her voice as she said, "Yes. From your cousin, Piers, whom I met and knew for a while in Sydney."

"Exactly. Though 'whom I knew for a while in Sydney' is something of an understatement, wouldn't you say?"

16

Honor's gesture was that of brushing cobwebs from before her face. "What do you mean by that, Mr. Lord?" she demanded.

"I'd expect you to know. Hadn't you better call at Control for your message?"

"Yes, I will. But I *don't* know, and I resent your attitude –"

"*Get that message!*" His grip upon her arm, propelling her forward, was vice-like and though she stiffened against it, it held fast.

At Control he released her to go to the desk alone. But he waited for her return. "Well, what was it?" he asked.

"From Dr. Page, saying he has been called to a case, can't meet me, and asking me to take a taxi to my quarters at U.N.H."

"A taxi? That won't be necessary. I'll drive you myself."

Honor shook her head. "Thank you, but no. I'll take a taxi."

"You'll do nothing of the kind. I didn't ask the long arm of coincidence to throw us together. But since it has, it gives me the chance to say to Miss Honor Troy things which I've had spoiling for some time, and what better opportunity than now? Come –"

With which he turned on his heel, called for a porter, and as Honor watched her own cases being trolleyed along with his, she had no choice but to follow where he led.

At his car she hung back, making a last stand of rejection of him. "This is *not* necessary, Mr. Lord!"

He agreed laconically. "And how right you are. As

17

far as I'm concerned, it's imperative. Please get in."

She sat rigidly at his side, her first daze of bewilderment turned now to a burn of anger. He had chosen to start this coil of mysterious dudgeon against her. Let him unravel it in his own time. She would not, *would* not appeal to him, ask him why –!

She didn't have to. Suddenly, without turning his head her way, he remarked almost conversationally,

"No wonder you were so quick on the draw with your 'Circe' clue this afternoon. Rang some kind of bell in your conscience, did it? Or not? Tell me. I'd be interested to know."

She stared ahead, willing herself not to show her dismay. "And I'd be equally glad if you would stop accusing me in riddles," she snapped. "Making me guilty of something – I don't know what – as soon as I admitted to being myself, of having known your cousin and of having heard your name through him. What's wrong with that?"

"Put so, nothing," he allowed. "Put my way, which I think is more on beam, everything. And though you may not care for riddles, I think you must get the drift of my meaning in the Circe-Penelope connection. Yes?"

Honor was silent, working it out. At last she said, "If you're cruel enough and unjust enough, I think I do. You obviously know that Piers Sabre and I were close . . . in love – or so I thought. And you are saying that I did my best to keep him with me long after he should have come back to Grand'terre; *wanted* to come, and I wouldn't let him? Is that it?"

Coolly, "As far as it goes. Though it's not the whole
18

parallel, is it? After all, a bit of elasticity to a holiday flirtation is one thing. Deliberately keeping an engaged man dancing attendance for an overstay of months is another, wouldn't you agree?"

Piers engaged! Then that was why –! Momentarily Honor felt she might faint. The sensation passed. "You think I knew he was engaged to someone else? And knowing it, I persuaded him to stay on?" she demanded.

"So I understood from him after I had called Time to the whole shabby affair."

"It was *not* shabby! But it was you who interfered?"

"Someone had to, for his fiancée's sake."

"And when Piers came back to her, he blamed me for keeping him away? Well, believe it or not as you may, Mr. Lord – *this* happens to be the truth. I had no idea at any time that Piers wasn't free; I put no pressure on him to stay in Sydney, and when he left he had jilted me almost without a word. And if you can't accept that from me, then ask *him* please whether it wasn't so! Just ask him, that's all. And, though I never thought to want to see him again, since it has happened this way –" Honor's chin jerked up proudly – "ask him, preferably in front of me!"

Arnot Lord turned briefly to look at her. "Then if he had written you off, he didn't bolt straight back to you when he left the island again?"

"When he *left* – again? But his engagement? What –?"

"Broken off before he went – within an hour or two of his coming back. We've had no news of his whereabouts since. And as that, as you know, was all of six

19

months back, forgive me, won't you, if I say of your present manoeuvre to follow up your affair with him — what a pity you should be that much too late?"

Honor gasped. "By that, you're suggesting that I came to Grand'terre now, running *after* Piers? When he had turned me down? When —?" Sheer outrage choked her there.

Unarguably, "Well, you did come and you are here, aren't you?" her accuser retorted.

"Only by the chance of my new job, as I've told you!"

"Acting on a packet of secret orders, not to be opened until after your take-off for Grand-terre? Oh, come! You must have been given more margin of choice to refuse than that!" he scoffed.

"Very little."

"But enough — if you had wanted to refuse?"

"Perhaps, though to the heads of an organisation like U.N.H. one doesn't argue 'personal reasons' with much success."

"I doubt if you tried very hard. A posting which saved you a lot of anxious scheming in your pursuit of Piers must have looked heaven-sent. Surely?"

Honor allowed her silence to answer the overt insult she read into that. Then she said, "And supposing I agree with you that I *didn't* try very hard?"

Watching his profile, she saw him lift an eyebrow in apparent surprise. "I congratulate you on your candour," he said. "So I was right? You *had* no more pride of spirit than to snatch at the opportunity to come up with a man who had jilted you — just like that?"

As she shook her head, Honor tasted a moment of power. "I'm sorry, but you're wrong," she said.

"So?"

"Yes. I accepted this posting when I realised that it was a chance I couldn't afford to let pass, and also because, in an island of the size and population of Grand'terre, there seemed no reason at all why I need fear any contact with Piers Sabre, *or* with such of his family as he had told me about."

"Not? In a single-citied island, and in a close-knit European community where everyone knows everyone, if not personally, at least by repute? You really can't ask me to believe that in the months of your torrid affair with Piers, you didn't learn enough about the set-up here to guess pretty certainly that you might meet him or one or other of us sooner or later!" Arnot Lord scorned. "For instance – his twin, his aunt, me, his fiancée –"

"I tell you, Piers never let me guess he had obligations to any other girl than me!" Honor flared.

"Though when he walked out on you, wasn't that the one obvious guess to make?"

She bit her lip. "I did wonder then. But I had no intention of trying to find out."

At that Arnot Lord glanced at her again, this time with an air of calculation. Looking front once more, he said, "You know, Miss Troy, even in face of my cousin's word to me that you did know he was engaged, and didn't care, I'd be inclined to believe you, *if* it weren't for a pretty damaging piece of evidence against!"

"*What* evidence against? What do you mean?"

21

"If I'm right, I think you'll know very soon." He broke off to nod ahead to where, at the end of a broad avenue into which he had turned the car, a pair of huge wrought-iron gates stood wide. "The main entrance to the U.N.H. plant," he said. "Do you know where you have to go?"

"No."

He took the car at a sweep through the gateway. "No matter. I think I do. At a hunch, you'll be sharing quarters with your housemate at that corner-bungalow over there."

Honor looked where he indicated, across shaded lawns towards a scatter of neatly thatched, verandahed dolls' houses set at small garden distance from each other. "*That* one?" she puzzled. "But how do you know?"

Driving the car at walking-pace now, he brought it to a halt at the door of the bungalow in question before he replied.

Then he said, "Because this is where my cousin Dorice Sabre lives on her job, and she happens, I know, to be expecting a new housemate from Sydney today. She hadn't been told your name, I think. Someone's oversight, that. But not too difficult to put the proverbial two and two together and make of them the evidence I spoke of just now – h'm?"

Honor stared at him aghast. "You mean you think *I* knew I should be sharing quarters with Piers Sabre's sister? That I snatched at the chance which that gave me to come in search of Piers? That I've been lying all along –?" she choked, her voice drowned by the long blast on his horn which was his only reply.

22

As she realised he meant it to, it brought from the bungalow a pretty, dark curly-haired girl so like to Honor's memory of Piers that a knot of pain caught at her heart.

The girl looked questioningly from Arnot Lord to Honor and back again. "What are *you* doing here?" she asked him in a voice just touched, no more, with a French inflection as Piers's had been.

Her cousin was out of the car now, lifting out Honor's cases, opening the door for her to alight. Over his shoulder as he did so, he said to Dorice,

"By the chance which threw your new colleague and me together on the plane. At Touton she got a message that her chief couldn't meet her, so I brought her out." Sketching a gesture of introduction between them, he added, "Dorice – Miss Honor Troy," and then, casually, of Honor's luggage, "Shall I put these things inside?"

Dorice said, "Oh, thanks. What a coincidence, the two of you meeting like that –!" while Honor stood ... waiting ... reading the girl's belated reaction to her name which had to come.

But to her utter amazement it did not. Instead there was Dorice's sunny smile, her easy, friendly, "Welcome to Grand'terre, Honor!" and her outstretched hand which Honor grasped and held in blind gratitude that it should be offered to her.

Drowning in bewilderment, she sensed rather than knew when Arnot Lord drove away. She didn't understand! If he knew her name from Piers, why didn't Dorice know it too? And since he knew it, and doubted and despised her as he surely did, why hadn't he betrayed her to Dorice as soon as they met?

Just that cool introduction of her, no more! Why, judging her so cruelly as he had himself, had he ever let her get so far as to meet Dorice at all? *Why*?

And why did it matter so much that at all costs — somehow — she had to know?

CHAPTER II

In the meanwhile Dorice's welcome was as practical as it was cordial.

She carried Honor's bags further into the tiny hall, opened doors, introduced rooms – "Our living salon; your bedroom, mine, with the bathroom doings between us; the kitchen, and a verandah at the back. All very twee and streamlined and the exact mate to all the other unmarried staff quarters – I daresay you'd like to freshen up and unpack a bit before tea, wouldn't you? Then we'll talk; get acquainted. Though I daresay you already know more about me than I do about you – through what Arnot must have told you, I mean? Of *all* the odd things, that you should have come in by the same flight! Odder still that the high-ups here wished you on to me as a housemate, without even telling me your name!"

Honor said, "The Sydney high-ups posted me here at very short notice. I was supposed to go somewhere else. They were in such a hurry to bundle me off that they didn't tell me your name either. Only Dr. Page's."

Dorice nodded. "Ah – Adam. You'll like him. But you won't meet him until tomorrow. He's gone up-country on a case and won't be back until late, I think. If you want anything, just shout –"

Honor's room was small but, even at that hour, cool behind its drawn slatted blinds. For some time after Dorice had left her alone in it, she stood aimlessly, looking at it but not seeing it, the turmoil of her thoughts elsewhere. Then, pulling herself together by a sheer effort of will, she showered and changed and went out to the verandah beyond the living-room where a dark-skinned Kanaka boy was laying a table for tea.

Dorice spoke to him in French, introduced him in English. "He manages in both," she told Honor. "We share his services with a couple of middle-aged German analytical chemists, so his cooking has to be pretty cosmopolitan – isn't that so, Koni-Mel?"

Though clearly not understanding "cosmopolitan", Koni-Mel nodded and grinned agreeably, flashing white teeth. "Me good cook," he asserted complacently. "What for the ma'ams for dinner tonight?"

Dorice said, "Nothing tonight. I'm taking Ma'am Troy out." As she poured China tea, she explained to Honor, "In *beech-la-mar*, which is pidgin-European, part-French, part-English, married or single we are all 'ma'ams' and all men employers are 'mastars', with an 'a', not an 'e'." Stirring her own tea, she went on, "And now for the autobiography bit from both of us. You know, I confess I did rather *dread* you. Without a name, you hadn't a face either. You might have been forty or a gargoyle, anything. But we fit, don't we? About the same age? Twenty? What are you?"

"Just twenty-one."

"And – what is the word? – foils to each other in our looks. My face, round and chubby, and yours, sort of triangular ... heart-shaped. I like your hair too, and the way you wear it – tucked behind each ear ... little girl-wise. You're so fair, you could be English –"

Honor smiled. "I am."

"You are? Not Australian? Tell –?" Dorice invited.

Carefully Honor sketched in her background and the circumstances which had brought her to Grand'-terre. Here and there Dorice put in a question or two which weren't too difficult to answer with truth. Then Dorice said, "Well, now about me. Though I daresay Arnot – he's my cousin, you know – put you into a lot of the picture while he was delivering you?"

"Yes. I was surprised he knew where to bring me, until he told me he had guessed I was the new house-mate he knew you were expecting. Do you work for Dr. Page too?"

"Oh no. I'm secretary to one of the top brass, a Monsieur Quien. It helps that I'm a bit bi-lingual, you see. Because I'm French-born, though by now I'm more at home in English, through having mostly spoken it for years at La Voile – but Arnot will have told you what the set-up is there, I suppose?"

Despising an evasion which was only just short of a lie, Honor said, "Yes, I know about your home, La Voile. That you lost both your parents when you were little and have lived there since with your aunt, Mr. Lord's mother. How long have you been working for U.N.H.?"

"About five months. Soon after Piers –" Dorice checked. "You know about Piers too?"

"He is your twin brother, isn't he?"

A nod. "Arnot told you? And about Ysanne?"

Though she could guess at the answer, Honor was able to put a near-genuine question. "Ysanne? She is –?"

"*Was* Piers' fiancée. She lives with us too. Ysanne Faudron, an orphan, like Piers and me. She's nineteen now, and she'd been engaged to Piers for nearly a year when he went on vacation to Sydney and tangled with some harpy there who wouldn't let him come back. Arnot told you about that?"

Guardedly, Honor said, "He mentioned that your brother had left home about six months ago."

"Yes, well – when Arnot pulled rank on him and threatened to stop his funds from the estate, he did come back. But only for a few hours, long enough for a blazing row with Arnot and to break with Ysanne before he left again, probably back to that woman. He –" Dorice's bright eyes shadowed – "he refused even to *see* me or Tante Rachel. And afterwards Arnot said it would be kindest to Ysanne if we all agreed to – to write him off, to try not to discuss him again. So we did, and not long after that I got the chance of this job and took it. It – makes it easier, you see, not to have to remember Piers at La Voile all the time."

Honor murmured, "Yes, I can understand that." For a moment her compassion for the other girl was tempted to the bald truth of "If it helps at all, Piers didn't go back to 'that woman'; he jilted her too." But once embroiled in the lie which had been forced on her, she resolved to act her despicable part in it until she had put to Arnot Lord that "Why?" to which she meant to have an answer. Sincerely she added to Dorice, "I'm sorry. But I dare say it helps that you're working?"

Dorice agreed, "Oh yes. I've got a lot of friends and I go about a lot. It's just that the – the dull ache of missing Piers is always there. Though even that must be worse for Ysanne, however brave a front she puts on, and she does that so well that you could almost believe she didn't care – Anyway, I'd rather thought that if you and I got on at all with each other, I'd take you out to La Voile for dinner tonight. Will you come?"

Honor drew a swift, aghast breath. *"Tonight?* Oh – !" (To meet Arnot Lord again; to meet Piers Sabre's aunt, perhaps his fiancée, to be exposed to them both as well as to Dorice, his twin! She wasn't *ready*. She couldn't! And yet, since it must be faced –!) Aloud she went on, "I mean, oughtn't I to report to someone, even though Dr. Page isn't here?"

"At this hour, no one to report to," Dorice said briskly. "Unless we're up to our eyes in work, we all take siesta hours off. No, there's nothing professional you can do until the morning. So I'll just ring Tante Rachel to say we'll be over. It's only about half an hour's run by car."

When she rejoined Honor, saying they needn't set out yet, Honor kept to the safe ground of asking her for details about the U.N.H. plant. "Mr. Lord warned me –"

Dorice cut in, "Oh, 'Arnot', for goodness' sake, please!"

"Well, he said that the smelting shops and the chimneys rather marred the tropical view. But all this –" Honor indicated their immediate surroundings – "is pleasant enough. Where *are* the actual works?"

"Way back, out of sight. And they're not as bad as all that. Down here, and in the executive offices and in your clinic, you can only just hear the hum of the machinery, that's all."

"And is Dr. Page resident on the plant or not?"

"Resident. He isn't married. His bungalow almost adjoins the clinic. But he has a cook-boy to himself. He doesn't have to share."

"And you think I shall like him?"

"Why, surely. And has *he* been sweating on the top line, waiting for you? *Has* he? I'll say –! Piles of work waiting for you, I understand. No boy for the paper work, our Adam; just a pretty grand doctor and that's enough," was Dorice's emphatic reply.

When they set out later for the drive to La Voile, Honor realised how little she had noticed on the journey in from the airport. Now Dorice pointed out some landmarks, telling her where to look towards the long "backbone" of the central mountain chain and promising her glimpses of the protecting barrier of the coral reef before they were out upon the coast road with the lagoon-calm sea in full view.

As they approached La Voile there was no view of the house.

It stood back from the palm-lined road, its foreground shaded by a spreading flame-of-the-forest tree in full crimson flower. It was a white ranch-style house with a roofed verandah running the length of its frontage. It looked cool and welcoming in the greenish early evening light.

Dorice parked her car alongside Arnot's, standing out, then shepherded Honor towards the house.

The black-and-white tesselated hall was empty, the rest of the house quiet as they went in. But a Kanaka girl in a maid's frilled apron hurried from the back of the hall at sight of them.

"Ma'am Dorice! You come 'long dinner tonight?" she beamed.

Dorice smiled back. "Two of us, Molla. Where is Ma'am Lord? And Mastar?"

"Ma'am in siesta. Mastar 'long garden, I think." Indicating a garden door opening off the hall, Molla scuttled away as a movement on the broad stairway caused both girls to look up. Dorice lifted a hand, calling, "Tante Rachel! We've arrived," and Honor stood silent and watchful of the woman who was coming down the stairs. (How much did she know? Or, if, like Dorice, nothing earlier, how much had she learned from her son since he came home?)

She was tall and sparsely built; her dark hair touched with grey, bouffant in an Edwardian style, her face rather gaunt and her nose as high-bridged as her son's.

"Ah, Dorice," she said. They touched cheeks in greeting, then calmly Mrs. Lord offered her hand to Honor as to any stranger. "And you, my dear, are –?"

Dorice supplied, "Honor. Honor Troy, though she hadn't got a name until she actually arrived. That is, as far as I was concerned. Adam Page hadn't told me."

Mrs. Lord smiled. "Honor?" She gave it a French inflection. "That is nice – a noble name. Welcome to Grand'terre and to La Voile," she said, and then to Dorice, "Some friends of hers have taken Ysanne to the Yacht Club for the evening, so she won't be in. But Miss Troy must meet Arnot, who is back. While I was resting, I heard his car."

31

So the danger was not over! Son and mother hadn't met yet. As panic swept Honor, she heard Dorice say, "Ah, but they have met – Honor and Arnot. They came in off the same flight from Sydney. They got acquainted on the plane, and he delivered her to me." Then the garden door opened, and Arnot Lord came across the hall.

Honor thought they must all hear the thudding of her heart. *Now* –! But though through a kind of mist she saw his heavy lids drop once, then lift from eyes which were still hard and accusing, mercifully – for the moment only? – he betrayed nothing of what he knew. For some reason he had drawn her into conspiracy with him. Again – *why?*

He acknowledged her with a cool, "So Dorice has lost no time in making you at home?" apparently as ready to welcome her as his mother had been.

After that Honor realised she was talking, moving, listening, even laughing with enough sincerity to conceal her tension within. She was shown the gardens, the rest of the house, the view from the back lawns towards the distant dark green of some of the estate's plantations. Guardedly she answered questions about herself and the work she had come to do; heard Piers' name in passing – "He is away from home just now," was the fiction her hostess told her, and managed to ask, even of Arnot Lord, her enemy, some interested questions of her own.

Though she was careful of allowing him to hold her glance for more than a second or two, once or twice she found herself studying his face in repose and in profile as she had done on the aircraft, though now seeking some family resemblance to Piers.

It wasn't there. Piers had been as dark as his twin, his nose small and delicate, his mouth mobile – petulant as a child's when he was annoyed or frustrated. By contrast, in Arnot's features there was a rugged strength and, resent him as she did, she envied any woman who, now or in the future, could rely on it, shelter behind it. A man whom it would be good to have on one's side . . .

Were there women in his life? Or one woman? almost certainly. But if he knew what it was to love, why had he been so contemptuous of her feeling for Piers? That was another question to which Honor found no answer.

They had drinks on a patio at the back of the house and dined in a gracious room at a shining rosewood table, waited upon with quiet efficiency by Molla. They had coffee at the table, then Dorice asked her aunt, "That silk I bought in the market for a housecoat – I left it here. I wonder, would you help me to cut it out?"

Mrs. Lord rose. "Now, dear?"

"Please. You'll see that I don't cut two sleeves for one arm, and I'd like to take it back with me when we go."

"Then of course. That is, if Honor" – Mrs Lord had slipped easily into using Honor's first name – "will excuse our running away. Arnot, take Honor back to the patio again, if it's still warm enough. Dorice and I won't be long."

But Arnot demurred, "It'll already be getting chilly. We'll adjourn to the salon." As he invited her to go ahead of him, Honor had no choice, though for the opportunity to demand of him what was the purpose of his silence about her, she would have preferred the dark of the patio where the only light was from a standard lamp of low power. In the brilliance of the elegant drawing-room she felt exposed. And when, after asking her permission to light a cigar, he chose to remain standing, his shoulders braced against a carved kingpost, his feet crossed easily at the ankles, he gained another advantage – that of some height above her chair.

He contemplated the tip of his cigar for a minute or two. Then he forestalled her.

"Evidently you took your cue from me, keeping your identity from Dorice. But you came tonight, prepared for a dramatic showdown, only to find that no one reacts to your name as I did, and you are burning to know why they don't?" he remarked.

She was glad to be able to shake her head. "No, I guessed that if your cousin didn't know my name, the rest of your family might not either. This afternoon Dorice talked about Piers –"

"Telling you things you already knew."

"Of course. Though showing me too that he probably hadn't named me to anyone but you."

"Which caused you to wonder what I meant to do about you?"

Honor met his downward glance unflinchingly. "I'm not merely wondering, Mr. Lord. I'm *demanding* of you why you kept my identity from Dorice."

"And now from my mother? M'm, a fair question, that."

"Then please answer it. Though that you acted out of generosity towards me is naturally the last thing I expect to hear!"

"Just as well, since I doubt if I'd indulge mere chivalry unless it happened to coincide with interests of my own."

"And they are –?"

"My family's interests – my mother's, Dorice's, Ysanne Faudron's. Your guess was right. I was the only person to hear your name from Piers. To the others I'm afraid you've always appeared as featureless, nameless trash, not worth their curiosity. Even Ysanne, I think, has had courage enough to cut her losses and put the affair behind her, and I decided that the past is the past and should be left to lie. There's no possible good to come of cutting down again to wounds that have healed. And so –"

"I see," Honor said slowly. "And now?"

"Ah, now I need your co-operation. Do I get it? Or could you be looking forward to the high drama of exposure? The kind of scene which could only give a lot of pain and make your position here quite impossible, unless you've a hide of leather. Well?"

Honor's chin went up. "Are you threatening me, Mr. Lord?"

"Merely forecasting what you can expect if you insist on the very letter of candour. What's more, if you insist on your big scene, do you know, I wonder, just how *I'm* going to see it?" As he spoke he moved away to flick cigar-ash into a tray, forcing Honor to address his back as, through dry lips, she questioned, "No. How?"

He turned then. "Simply," he said, "as your petty comeback at Ysanne, paying her out for her having owned Piers before you did. Or even more meanly –" his gesture checked Honor as, outraged, she sprang to her feet – "throwing in her face your triumph in having purloined him from her. If I can suspect that of you, others may. And as I've told you – we're a tight little community; we hang together, and what the wagging tongues could do to your reputation, I leave you to guess."

Honor drew herself up. "You *are* threatening me!" she stated.

He nodded. "If you like. But go ahead. *Bare* your conscience. *Give* pain to innocent people. Collect blame that I'm offering you the chance to avoid –" Suddenly he ground the glow of his cigar to dead ash and covered the distance between them in a couple of strides. Gripping her shoulder, he swung her about to face a free-standing gilt-framed mirror which showed both their figures full length.

"Look there," he ordered savagely. "You've got dimension, shape, attractions, haven't you? You're not nameless. You're not featureless. That's some other girl. . . . You are Honor Troy, a newcomer from your own background, free to make your own appeal to people. Since *my* interests and *your* good happen to dovetail, you don't have to be more of a reckless little fool than you need. As long as you hold your tongue and I hold mine, you can continue to be yourself – without strings." His grip still fast, again he added, "Well?"

Dimension. Shape. Attractions. From any man less

36

intent on his own purposes, his mention of them might have been compliments, Honor thought as she stared into the mirror, stung by his taunts but aware that she was yielding to the compulsion of his reason. And to something more. Something she saw, though only vaguely, as a need to stand well with him, to make him believe in her good faith, to have him on her side. At last she said, "You make it very difficult not to agree. Very well, I'll – hold my tongue."

"Good." He released her shoulder and as her own hand went instinctively to it, as if to guard it from him, he smiled thinly.

"You remind me," he said, "of a child wiping off the kiss of an obnoxious grown-up. Are you going to find your enforced alliance with me as uneasy as all that?"

"It depends on what you make of it, I think," she said.

"I? You too, surely? Anyway, with Dorice as our linkman, it shouldn't be too difficult. We can meet without embarrassments, I hope. How long is your penal sentence, by the way?"

Understanding him, "Two years," she told him.

His brows lifted. "No reprieve for you in that time?"

"Yes. If for personal reasons I can't settle, I can apply for a transfer at the end of six months."

"And you'll be taking advantage of that?"

Honor looked straight at him. "In the circumstances, need you ask?" she said, experiencing the puny satisfaction of having the last word as Mrs. Lord and Dorice rejoined them.

Soon after they had taken to the road on their return journey, Dorice said, "A pity Ysanne was out. Then you'd have met the whole bunch of us – except Piers."

"Yes. It was good of Mrs. Lord to make me welcome as she did. What is Ysanne Faudron like?"

"Oh – well, she is a tiny little thing even darker than I am, and with a lovely olive skin, instead of freckles, like me. Rather doll-like and appealing – you know, the kind that women pat on the shoulder, saying 'There, there!' and men seem to yearn to protect. The fey, faerie type – you know?"

Honor nodded. "I think so. Do you like her?"

Dorice shrugged. "We get along now. I even find myself doing some 'There, there', stuff myself on occasion, and though I was madly jealous of her when Piers fell for her, I was just about as mad with *him* when he took up with that Australian wench, and only came back to leave Ysanne flat."

"How long has she lived at LaVoile?"

"For about two years. She came out here from France with her stepfather, who was a kind of remittance man. He drove his car over a cliff one night when he had been drinking, which left Ysanne as a bit of driftwood. So Tante Rachel took her on as her companion. That was when Ysanne was seventeen. Neither Piers nor I wanted her, but after a while he got fascinated, and when it dawned on me why Tante Rachel wanted her, I didn't mind so much."

"Why did Mrs. Lord want her?"

"I'm pretty sure – as the daughter she had never had."

Honor considered that. "But hadn't she had you –

since you and Piers were small?" she queried.

Dorice shook her head. "Never – in the way she had, and still has Ysanne, who is biddable and charming and rewarding to dress and take about. The perfect home-girl, which I never was. I think Tante Rachel was over-joyed when she and Piers got engaged. It meant that she would be keeping Ysanne as a daughter, and I be-lieve she hopes that may still happen, though by way of Arnot instead."

"You mean that your cousin and Ysanne –?"

"Oh, there's nothing definite between them. It's only my idea. After all, he is years older than she is. He is thirty; she is just nineteen. But she can twist him any way she wants, and he is as protective of her as we all are – especially since Piers let her down. Anyway, when he decamped, that brought Ysanne and Tante Rachel closer, and that gave me my chance to fly the nest. I've got a small income of my own, and when I've worked a bit longer and saved some more, I'm really off and away."

"Off? Where?"

"Travelling. Seeing the world. Working my way if I have to – as I almost certainly shall." Momentar-ily Dorice lifted both hands from the wheel and spread them wide. "Europe, America, Asia – here I come!" she declaimed.

Honor smiled her sympathy. "Good for you! I hope you make it. But is marriage no part of your plans?"

Dorice tilted her head in thought. Then, "Certainly not in my *plans*," she said. "But is it ever? I mean, you see it happening all over. A girl is heartwhole to-day and down for the count to some man tomorrow, and after that, marriage is the only logical outcome, isn't it?"

"Always supposing they both went down for the count for each other," Honor said quietly.

"Ah well, that's different, of course," Dorice agreed. "Too many girls, eating out their hearts for men who don't throw a glance their way. I'm lucky. It hasn't happened to me yet. Nor to you?"

Honor hesitated before deciding she could tell a partial truth. "Not exactly," she said. "But I've been jilted once."

Dorice said quickly, "Oh, I'm sorry. I didn't know. I hope there's been someone else for you since?"

Honor shook her head. "No one as yet."

"Not even any other man who has interested you? You know how it happens, even before you've learned much about them? You look at them, and wonder about them . . . a bit intrigued. Or hasn't there been time for you to feel interested since your other affair?"

Honor drew a long breath. "Probably not enough time," she said, though she was aware of a pulse of thought which denied the words.

CHAPTER III

THE surgery, a white one-storeyed building, was adjacent to Dr. Page's quarters, separated by a strip of well-worn lawn. It comprised an outer office where Honor would work, a consulting-room, a rest-cubicle and a tiny dispensary, stocked with the more homely remedies and bandages.

Honor went across to it early, while the Kanaka cleaning-woman was still at work and before her chief arrived. The woman looked a question at her as she opened the door and went in, but smiled and nodded a welcome when Honor put on the white linen coat she had been carrying over her arm.

The door marked "Dispensary" was locked. The other doors stood ajar, but Honor confined her attention to her own sphere – the desk, the filing-cabinets and the row of three or four chairs which indicated that the office doubled as a waiting-room for patients.

She was examining the typewriter, testing it for touch with the hoary "Quick brown fox ..." exercise, when Dr. Page arrived. He was acknowledged by the cleaner on her way out as "Mastar Doctor," and came forward to the desk, offering Honor his hand.

She would have been blind, to be unaware of the approval of her which smiled at her from the light blue eyes in the fair boyish face of her new chief. Since he was qualified, he must be at least in his late twenties, but he appeared no older than she was, she was thinking as he pump-handled her hand and breathed,

"So I've achieved you at last – after three months of nagging, and local temps who haven't known the difference between a syringe and a typewriter eraser! Sorry I couldn't meet you at Touton; would have given us the chance to get acquainted off-duty, so to speak. However, that's something in store, and Dorice Sabre, nice child, coped all right, I hope?"

Honor smiled. "Excellently. She insisted on taking me to her home for dinner, to meet her people."

"To La Voile? Did she indeed?" Adam Page queried. " 'Fraid I don't know them well myself, except to nod to Arnot Lord at the Club, by his repute as a bit of an autocrat, and through the odd call to one of his estate workers. Not part of our chore, of course, but the city panel of medics and I do locum for each other when necessary; could happen that I'm called anywhere then. Anyway, what was *your* impression of the man?"

Honor ran a slim forefinger along the edge of the desk. "Oh, I don't know. Perhaps just a fleeting idea that, as you suggest, he is an autocrat; very sure that he'll be obeyed."

"M'm – *in* working-hours as well as out of them, or so one hears –" As Adam Page spoke, he crossed to his surgery; back at its open door a minute later – "Show you round, shall I? And brief you, before the patients, if any, arrive?" he suggested.

A quarter of an hour or so later Honor understood at least the rudiments of her duties, some of which went beyond those of a secretary-cum-filing clerk.

She would not have to dispense, but she must stock-check the dispensary regularly and would be responsible for the re-ordering necessary. Usually she would man the surgery in Dr. Page's absence, though she would be free when the surgery, like the other executive offices, closed for the siesta hours. For the rest, she would keep the filing and index-card systems, write letters, answer the telephone and accompany her chief on his rounds when he needed her.

Honor queried this latter, "What happens to the telephone when neither of us is here?"

"You switch through, and any calls are taken in one of the main 'shops' and reported back. You have to accompany me on occasion, because, as you know, we attend the families of all the U.N.H. personnel, as well as the men themselves. This means that when the patient is the wife or daughter of a Kanaka worker, their rather strict taboos demand that I be chaperoned, and so must take you along," Dr. Page explained.

The first patient of the morning arrived just then – his trouble, the emergency of a cut wrist. The next man was on his second visit for a laryngeal condition; the third man wanted a chit for a surgical boot. The telephone rang frequently; reference cards had to be produced and filed, but it was all a fairly familiar pattern of business to Honor after her Sydney experience. But one contretemps floored her when she answered the telephone to a stream of rapid French, only about one word in six of which she understood, and had, to her shame, to call in her chief as interpreter.

She listened in to his side of the exchange, finding his more leisurely French with an English accent much easier to understand. From his glance down at her as he perched on the edge of her desk, she knew he was explaining who she was to the caller, and a minute later he covered the mouthpiece to say in English,

"Jean Salinger, a boffin friend of mine from the Lab. Has a new girl, apparently so dewy that she won't go out with him tête-à-tête, so he wants me to square the party at the Yacht Club tonight with another woman. I wonder, would you let me take you along?"

Honor hesitated. "Thank you very much, but— That is, I don't know whether my housemate may have made some plans for me."

"Well, if she has, that's all right. Another time— But for now may I say yes to Jean provisionally and get him off the line?"

She nodded her consent, making a mental note to ask Dorice what one did on an evening at the Yacht Club, what one wore. Replacing the receiver, Adam Page commented, "Another dumb blonde for Jean. How he does collect them, I will say! Usually so young that they want to bring their mamas along, and if you asked him the name of the one he was escorting last week, he wouldn't know."

Honor laughed dutifully, but was worrying over a problem of her own.

She said, "I told the V.I.P.s in Sydney that I had hardly any French to my name. And though they brushed it off as if it didn't matter, what do I do when *that* happens—" she nodded meaningly at the telephone — "and it could be an important call, and you might not be here?"

"Ah – Well, you keep your head, wait for a pause in the flow, then say 'Speak English, if you please', – and they will."

"Always?"

"Almost. They're a bi-lingual lot on Grand'terre, you'll find. Among the Europeans, so many mixed marriages between French and English for several generations, that the children grow up, speaking both from birth. Take your housemate, for instance – the Sabres and the Lords; both French one side and English the other. That's typical, and I daresay Dorice will chatter French to you for practice any time you ask. Alternatively, you could always spend your evenings curled up with a good French grammar, a pile of language records and a wholesome cup of cocoa," Adam Page advised, adding gallantly as he returned to his room, "Though that's something I doubt if you'll find time for, once you're in circulation. Better keep it conversational after all – you'll learn more and get further that way."

Presently he went out on his rounds of the factory "shops" and on some family visits, suggesting before he went a time for calling for Honor in the evening, and asking her to ring his bungalow – his cook would take a message – if she couldn't keep their date.

After he had gone Honor checked the stock in the dispensary with its inventory, finding that whoever had last done that chore hadn't seen to it that the items tallied. Correcting and searching and making a new inventory of all that was physically on the shelves took her what was left of the morning until the the works siren blared the signal for the siesta break, setting her free for the afternoon.

Dorice had told her overnight that after laying their table and preparing their usually cold luncheon food, Koni-Mel would then leave to attend to his German clients, shuttling back later to see to their dinner. But back at the bungalow Honor found only one place laid in the coolly shuttered living-room – for her alone, she gathered from the note which she found propped against the telephone.

Koni-Mel's message began respectfully, "Ma'am Troy . . ." followed that with the luncheon menu, in its turn followed by his relay of Dorice's own message to her – "Ma'am Sabre not come. Ma'am Troy to please take *déjeuner* alone" – and concluded with a "Good-bye for now, ma'am", which his second thoughts had evidently prompted him to overscore in favour of a more formal, "Good morning".

The midday heat was now intense. Too hot, Honor decided after eating pleasurably from the dishes she found awaiting her in larder and refrigerator, for anything more active than an hour's rest on her bed – a practice which in Sydney she knew she would have scorned as a wilful waste of time, but which here she supposed she would indulge as a rather sensible "must".

Not meaning to, she fell asleep in the darkened room; woke, showered and was wondering when she could expect Dorice to return, when a small car drove up and halted outside. Not Dorice's car, which still stood where she had parked it last night. The newcomer was a neat cream three-wheeler, upholstered in blue with its top open to the sun; its driver a very young girl whom Honor's instinct recognised at sight.

Ysanne Faudron. Piers' girl, as tiny and graceful as Dorice had described her. She and Honor met halfway between the car and the door of the bungalow, each offering a hand. In English, in a light little voice slightly more accented than Dorice's, the other girl said, "We didn't meet last night. I am Ysanne – Ysanne Faudron," and then, as she released Honor's hand, "What is the matter? You are cold?"

"Cold? In this heat?"

Ysanne shrugged and smiled. "Silly question. It was just that your wrist trembled – You are Honor Troy, of course. Odd, wasn't it, how you and Arnot met on the flight from Sydney, and only discovered your connection with Dorice after you arrived? Anyway, where is Dorice? Is she in? Not? Oh well, it was just that she left part of her dressmaking behind last night, and I brought it over."

Back at her car, Ysanne took a parcel from it, saying over her shoulder, "How do you like my little car? She is rather new, and I'm still at the stage where I'll make any excuse for driving her."

Honor went forward to touch the shining paint-work. "She is very chic," she said.

"Isn't she? Arnot gave her to me for my nineteenth birthday." Ysanne smiled disarmingly, "Do you know, now I'm here, I wouldn't refuse a cup of tea?"

"You'd like one? And you'll stay until Dorice comes in?" Honor asked.

"It depends on how long she is likely to be. I've a date for tonight. But I'll wait for a while."

47

They went together to prepare the tea, and took it out to the patio where it was now cool enough to sit. They exchanged commonplaces, then Ysanne asked, "How do you like Dorice?"

"Very much," said Honor. "I'm lucky to have her for a housemate. She made me welcome from the start."

"I'm glad. And she must have liked you too, or she wouldn't have raced you over to La Voile on your first night here." Ysanne stirred her tea thoughtfully. "But then you two would get on, wouldn't you? You're both the restless, adventurous sort, aren't you? You are English, but you emigrated to Australia, and now you're taking Grand'terre in your stride –"

"I only went to Sydney because my people emigrated, and I came to Grand'terre on my job –" Honor pointed out.

Ysanne brushed the interruption aside. "And Dorice can't wait to get away. But if she hopes to pick up a husband on her way round the world, she could be disappointed. Everyone knows that most shipboard and holiday romances end the same way – in tears. Don't you agree?"

Honor winced at the innocently put question. "Perhaps," she agreed. "Though I gather Dorice's ambition *is* only a world tour, without romance in mind."

Ysanne wrinkled her pretty nose. "Ah, so she *says*. But isn't it always at the back of any girl's mind? Confess now – it is at yours?"

Honor shook her head. "I don't think so."

"I only said – at the *back* of your mind!"

"Not even there. I like men and I keep dates, but for

48

the time being I'm very contented with my job. Aren't you with yours?"

"With mine?" Ysanne's echo was blank, then she laughed softly. "Oh, of course! Dorice will have told you I'm Mrs. Lord's companion. But really it's not like that any more. I call her Tante Rachel, as Dorice does, and as she would really have been if –" Ysanne broke off to raise darkly troubled eyes to Honor's – "I suppose Dorice will have told you about Piers and me?" she appealed.

"That you were engaged to her twin brother? Yes, I knew that. I'm – sorry."

As she spoke Honor experienced guilt – the guilt of the unfair advantage afforded by superior knowledge which could not be shared. It was rather as if, through no right of her own, she had been put one move ahead in a game of skill, and for a moment she found herself tempted to speak the very few words which would allow Ysanne to draw level – whatever the consequences to herself.

She remembered her hot resentment of Arnot Lord's suggestion that she might indulge a petty revenge by telling Ysanne the truth. But she hadn't reckoned then with the impulse of honesty which she had felt just now – though forced to let it pass because of the promise she had given him to keep silent.

Ysanne's little-girl voice broke into her thoughts. "So you'll know too about the fool Piers made of himself with some girl he picked up in Sydney; who, once she got her hooks into him, wouldn't let go? After all, I had trusted him. I thought he knew how to be loyal to me. But after I – that is, when our engagement was broken and he left home, I knew Arnot was right to advise me to forget him. It was difficult. I was terribly shocked. But it helped that at least Arnot knew I was trying hard to be generous. He said so."

"And Piers – your fiancé – had told Mr. Lord how it had all happened?" Despising the question, Honor had felt forced to ask it.

"I suppose so. I didn't want to hear the details, though I daresay this girl made scenes and threatened all kinds of dramatics if he left her. And of course she knew that if she could keep him she was –" Ysanne hesitated before the slang English phrase – "she was on to a good thing". "I daresay he went back to her when he left here. Nobody knew," Ysanne concluded.

But somebody did know. Arnot Lord did, thought Honor, hurt to her core that Piers hadn't been man enough to tell the truth which would have saved her from Arnot's bitter judgement of her part in the affair. Couldn't Piers have taken his family's censure without sheltering behind "the woman tempted me"?

She saw that Ysanne was standing now, preparing to leave. In the driving-seat of her car she looked like a fairy in a blue-and-white chariot, and as she switched on she looked up with a deprecating little smile.

"Do you know, this car was supposed to be a birthday present and a secret. In fact, on the morning of the day – it should have been my wedding morning, you see – Arnot only gave me the keys. But when the car was delivered, he told me, 'It's not only for your birthday, it's for courage as well.' My courage over Piers, he meant. I couldn't find anything to say. I just *kissed* him, for appreciating how hard I'd had to try

... to face up! Especially when I'd always thought he hadn't wanted Piers to marry me. Almost as if he were jealous of Piers over me. Which would be silly ... wouldn't it?" Her laughter rang out lightly and musically over the hum of the car as she drove away.

Watching her out of sight, Honor was puzzled as to her reaction to her. Curiosity was satisfied. Ysanne Faudron was all that Dorice had described – appealingly feminine to her fingertips; easily friendly and ingenuous. She took an understandable pride in having forgiven Piers, as Honor herself had; both of them looking forward now, not back. And yet nothing of the instant trust which had sprung between herself and Dorice had come through between her and Ysanne.

Why not? Her own fault? Or Ysanne's? Something said? Not said? Looked? Implied? On her own side it couldn't be jealousy or envy of Ysanne now. Or could it? Without any envy now of Ysanne's possession of Piers Sabre, did she grudge the girl the quality of sympathy which Arnot Lord had studiedly withheld from herself, even while co-opting her so that Ysanne should be saved pain?

Reluctantly Honor knew the answer was yes. She would give much to change places with Ysanne.

Dorice, arriving shortly afterwards, explained that her chief had issued a rare invitation to her to lunch with him. She was pleased that Honor had a date for the evening, as she also was to visit friends. Noticing the two tea-cups, she said, "You've been entertaining! Who?"

"Ysanne Faudron. She drove over to bring some stuff you left at home last night. I've put it in your room. She stayed to tea, and we got acquainted," Honor said.

"Ysanne? What did you think of her?"

"Well, I think you are right about her – she does appeal to one's protective instincts. She had mine when she told me about her broken engagement. But she talked quite naturally about your brother. She says she has forgiven him, and she is being brave about forgetting him too."

"M'm – cutting her losses, lucky wench. I wish I could do the same yet. I wonder what it is about twinhood that makes you feel a bit of yourself has been torn away, when the other half of you lets you down?" Dorice mused.

Pitying her, Honor said, "You don't think, then, that Piers will come back within some measurable time?"

Dorice shrugged. "How can one tell? I try to hope so, but – But you got the message from Ysanne that we all do; Arnot particularly. Namely that she is for cherishing and shielding from any old wind that blows. Well, thank goodness, no one ever felt that way about me. Being at the receiving end of people's loving charity must be awfully wearing, wouldn't you say?" She rose as she spoke. "Time for a little sundowner before we change. What will you have, and what are you going to wear for your date with Adam?"

They had enjoyed a cosy feminine get-together over clothes, Dorice approving Honor's choice of a green-and-white check silk dress and a poncho as a wrap. Now Adam Page had called for her on time, saying they were to meet the other two at the Yacht Club.

It was Honor's first sight of the Baie des Palmiers, where craft of all sizes and types rode at anchor in the fading evening light. The Yacht Club building, starkly white, its architecture pseudo-nautical with porthole windows to its ground floor and radio aerials on its roof, stood directly at the top of a broad slipway which went down to the water. From the number of parked cars and the crowds milling about its forecourt, it was evidently a favourite evening rendezvous for the city.

Jean Salinger proved to be a debonair type with a wicked wink and gesturing hands which spoke volumes. His latest girl, chubby with puppy-fat, was a New Zealander on holiday, whose wide-eyed gaze at Jean was the pure, unquestioning devotion of a spaniel. Watching her, hearing her shy contributions to the talk, Honor longed to warn her, *Don't care too much. You've so little time to impress yourself on him, and you could take months or years to forget*. In the meantime, they made a congenial party and were on their way to their table along an aisle of the vast red-curtained dining-room when their waiter, leading them, halted to make way for another couple.

"Thank you." The man's voice acknowledged the courtesy, but he did not move on as Honor saw he had noticed her, immediately behind the waiter. He said, "Well?" on a note of question, then, "so you're being initiated into our Yacht Club, Miss Troy?" and then to his young companion, "You two met each other this afternoon, didn't you?"

Ysanne's piquant little smile came and went. "Yes, didn't we, and got on famously? Though you" – she crooked an admonishing finger at Honor – "didn't say

53

you were dining here tonight. If you had, we could have made a party, the six of us."

At that Arnot said, "No reason why we shouldn't now, if you'd like to. Yes?"

The others agreed. Jean and his Eunice were introduced, and presently they gathered at a table for six. As Ysanne brushed past Honor's chair on her way to her own, she whispered roguishly, "Men – not even at the *back* of your mind? I must say it hasn't taken you long to change it!" Flushing against her will, Honor concentrated on her menu-card. For, looking up from it once, she had caught Arnot's glance studying her. Critically? Approving her poise in meeting Ysanne? She could not tell.

The party developed easily, though Eunice, for one, was plainly outclassed in face of Ysanne's spontaneous gaiety. For Ysanne sparkled – there was no other word for her light, adroit handling of all three men; provocative with Jean, claiming to be awed by Adam and deferring to Arnot on every subject which came up. Until, as they were about to adjourn for coffee in one of the lounges, her slim fingers rapped the table.

"No!" she declared. "I want to swim. Who else will come?" Her bright glance swept them all.

Jean spoke for himself and Eunice, "We didn't bring any gear." Adam said, "Nor did we." Arnot said peremptorily, "You're not swimming directly after dinner. And you can't – the pool has been emptied for cleaning."

Ysanne claimed, "But I didn't mean here. Who wants to swim indoors on a moonlight night? I want to go to Anse Sainte Marie. And I *am* prepared. I always

54

keep a swimsuit in my locker."

Arnot said, unmoved, "You are still not swimming tonight."

"Who says so?" she flouted him.

"I do. What's more, how do you propose to get to Sainte Marie? On foot?"

"Of course not. If you won't drive me, I'll take your car myself."

"How? I happen to have the keys. Here –" Almost lazily he produced a bunch from a pocket and laid it on his open palm.

What happened next was at a speed which brought exclamations from the others and a reflex closing of Arnot's hand which came a split second too late for Ysanne's pounce, as swift and sure as a kitten's claw upon a mouse.

Her eyes dark with mischief, she dangled the keys, making their clink audible even to the neighbouring tables, before she snatched up her bag, teased Arnot, "And who has them now, *mon ami*?" and ran, threading her way between waiters and tables until she disappeared.

Honor saw Arnot's lips set. He called for the waiter, signed a chit, then rose. "You'll excuse me?" He bowed slightly in the direction of Honor and Eunice and was gone.

Round about, the rustle of talk and laughter was resumed. Adam Page pursed his lips in a long-drawn "Phew – we!" and Jean Salinger asked of no one in particular, "And who, would you say, is going to win *that* round?"

They went for coffee, danced later and parted company at midnight, by which time the other two had not reappeared. On the way back Adam and Honor discussed the evening without mentioning them until Adam said into a silence, "And if you are asking me, I'd say that little cutie has all the makings of a tramp."

Honor gasped. "You mean Ysanne Faudron? Oh no! She was just being – young."

"Young?" Adam scoffed. "My dear girl, she's as old in guile as Cleopatra! Anyway, she doesn't believe in *wasting* men, that's for sure. She set out to make none of us feel safe – neither Jean nor me, and look at the fool she made of Lord! Though perhaps only for the moment, and it's my fervent hope that he saw she got the shaking she asked for."

Honor said slowly, "I agree she frivolled a lot at dinner. But that could be in self-defence."

"Self-defence from whom?"

"From – people. You'll know, of course, that Dorice's twin broke his engagement to her and left Grand'terre? So that perhaps she puts on this flirtatious front with men; daring them to hurt her again."

Adam's silence greeted that. Then he conceded, "Maybe, though she didn't strike me as being very heartlorn. However, you, being a woman, are on her side?"

"I think I understand," Honor said non-committally, then changed the subject to ask, "What – and where – is Anse Sainte Marie?"

"*Anse* is French for a cove. Sainte Marie is a little bay five or six kilometres west of Palmiers. Just a crescent of sand and palms and the lagoon water like warm silk, even at midnight. The Southern Pacific version of

Lovers' Lane, you might say. Which made our young friend's public luring of Arnot Lord into taking her there not all that subtle," concluded Adam with a grin.

Honor's smile in reply was stiff. "Would you say she succeeded?"

"Who knows? As Jean remarked, we were only treated to the opening moves. The play may have gone either way later. But of one thing I'm pretty sure – she never had any intention of taking that moonlight swim by herself!"

"She threatened she would."

But when Adam gave in with an easy, "O.K. The lady has no guile at all, and I don't know a hussy when I see one," Honor realised he had only confirmed her own doubts of Ysanne Faudron's sincerity, even while she envied the girl's success in eliciting whatever response she wanted from people.

According to Dorice, she had gained the mother-love of Mrs. Lord; she had Dorice's sympathy; this afternoon she had had Honor's own ready pity; she had Arnot Lord in thrall to her chameleon-coloured moods. Or was that his skill – letting her believe he was her puppet, when in fact both her deference and her defiance were tributes to a mastery which Ysanne dared to challenge only just so far?

If that were so, then he had won the small duel even before he had left the table to follow her. For Arnot, Honor suspected, was no woman's slave, except when it might suit his own ends to indulge her. So that, though Ysanne might get her moonlight swim after all, even she might not realise that it was at his will, not hers, that the game was being played his way.

CHAPTER IV

THE pattern of Honor's working days took a fairly regular, manageable shape; mornings spent in the clinic, clerical work which sometimes necessitated a return there after siesta, and the occasional need for her to play chaperon to Adam on family calls.

On these trips and during breaks in their work she and Adam got to know each other; explored the different ways which had brought them both to Grand'-terre; discussed a future which might take them from it in time.

Adam, Honor learned, was thirty. After qualifying in England, meaning to travel before going into general practice, he had studied tropical medicine, had joined U.N.H. as a medical officer and had been posted to Grand'terre as his first assignment.

"Your first?" Honor had queried. "You'll be moving on?"

"Oh yes. And when I've done with lotus-eating in the sun, I'll be going back. What about you? What's the length of your contract here?"

"For two years, with the option of leaving at the end of six months, if I wish."

"Don't you dare, if I'm still here!" Adam had threatened. "But if you stay for your full term, what then?"

"I shan't be staying."

"No permanent lotus-eating for you either? But

what if you married here?"

"That's not likely."

"Rubbish. How can you tell?" scoffed Adam, ignorant of the real reason why she could never hope for any "happy ever after" future on this lovely island. Between them, Piers Sabre and Arnot Lord had seen to that. But that was something she could not explain to Adam.

Meanwhile they dovetailed well as colleagues and met in the same friendly circles outside working hours. Both he and Dorice were on hail-fellow terms with a host of people, proving to Honor how right Arnot had been in scorning her idea that, in so hedged a community, she could have avoided any contact with Piers's family or his friends. Dorice almost always had something "on", and only when Honor claimed firmly that she needed time to herself was Dorice willing to go out without her.

It was on one such evening when Dorice had gone home to La Voile, that Honor, basking in the last of the sun on the patio, looked up from her book to see, first a long shadow, and then the figure of Arnot Lord coming round the side of the bungalow.

Surprised, Honor said, "Oh, I'm afraid Dorice is out. I believe she meant to go over to La Voile."

"Yes. She had arrived before I left. May I –?" As he spoke Arnot indicated an empty chair, waiting for Honor to reseat herself.

She remained standing. "May I get you a drink?" she offered.

He glanced at the empty rattan table. "Don't bother for me. I really came to see you."

"Me? Just – me?" As she sat down again, her heart thumped.

"Just you," he confirmed, "hoping to find you alone. I have to have your help."

"My help?" But Honor's echo, as blank as her first, was interrupted by the slam of the french door behind her chair, and Adam, in shorts and a T-shirt, a towel draped on a shoulder, stood on the sill.

The two men acknowledged each other with nods. Adam said, "Anyone for a swim? Like to come? The Club? Citrons? The Plage? Take your choice."

Honor shook her head. "Not tonight for me, and Dorice has gone home." She hesitated. "Mr. Lord and I weren't drinking, but if you'd like to, I daresay –?" She glanced with raised eyebrows at Arnot, who agreed coolly, "Very well." Upon which, as she was about to rise, Adam's hand came down on her shoulder.

"I'll do the necessary," he said. "Escort duty rejected; wine-waiter service on offer instead." With which he turned back into the house, only to reappear, dangling a jazzy pullover from a couple of fingers.

"Newly pressed *and* mended, to boot!" he commented.

Honor laughed. "What did you expect? When you lent it to me in Wednesday's downpour, it got thoroughly soaked, so could I do less than see it was in good order before I gave it back?"

Adam grinned. "A labour of love, I trust?"

"*Labour*, anyway. The right elbow was practically non-existent!"

"Well, remind me to take it when I go." He departed again on his errand, leaving Honor only too aware that her other guest found him *de trop*.

They listened to the chink of glasses, the slam of cupboard and refrigerator doors. Then Arnot commented, "You seem to be on comfortable domestic terms with Page – doing his mending and making him free of your kitchen arrangements."

Sensing criticism, Honor retorted, "Why not? They're twins – the kitchens, I mean, as all the bungalows are. Drawers, cupboards – the lot, to the very last cuphook –" Conscious that her babbling was making no case at all for Adam's ease in a house not his own, she let her voice trail away into a silence which lasted until he returned with a bottle of wine, the makings of some long drinks and a bowl of ice cubes.

"It's all right, I filled the tray again," he told Honor's glance at the latter, adding to Arnot, "These types, Honor and Dorice, are quite wanton in the matter of ice. Their freezing tray would never hold anything but luke water, if I didn't keep behind them, nag, nag, nag."

"Really?" Arnot's interest sounded as cool as the subject under discussion. He turned to Honor. "By the way, my mother is giving a small party for Ysanne on Sunday – nothing big, just dinner and talk – and she hopes you will come with Dorice and any friends you'd care to bring along. Can you come?"

(Was it this that he had come to say to her? Honor wondered.) Aloud she accepted, "Sunday? Yes, I'd like to, very much."

"You too, perhaps?" Arnot asked Adam.

"Thanks. Glad to, if I may put myself on call by

telephone at your house?" Adam said.

"Of course. I'll leave my mother to arrange times with Dorice."

The threesome talk went on diffidently. Adam seemed to have abandoned his plans to swim and Honor felt that each man hoped to sit the other out – Adam, because he was relaxed and at leisure after a taxing day; Arnot, she could only suppose, because he hadn't yet said what he had come to say, hoping to find her alone.

At last she broke up the party herself by preparing to move indoors. At which Adam – if there were any competition between them – gave Arnot best and departed, jauntily swinging his mended pullover and with a gay "See you –" to Honor.

Sensing atmosphere again, Honor resolved, "I will *not* apologise for him," and waited for Arnot to explain his errand.

He began without preliminary, "Yes, well – I take it I can depend on you to come to La Voile on Sunday?"

Surprised by the question, "Why, yes," she told him.

"Good. Because a certain man will be there whom I want you to meet. Or rather, confront might be a better word."

Honor frowned in perplexity. "A man I don't know? Confront him? Why?"

Arnot confirmed, "A man I hope you don't know; won't recognise and will be able to deny to his face that he can ever have seen you before."

"I – don't understand?"

"Then let me explain. The facts are these – I employ this man, Noel Bonner. He is one of our export salesmen of copra, and at some time or other while Piers Sabre was in Sydney, he was there too."

"In *Sydney*?"

Arnot nodded. "You've guessed it. He has seen you around – at the Yacht Club and other places, and the other day he mentioned to me in passing that he thought he had seen you before. At first he didn't sound too sure, but he convinced himself while he was talking. Yes, in Australia; in Sydney, in fact. And yes, he *believed* somewhere, he wasn't sure where, in the company of Piers . . . You see?"

"You mean that . . . that he could have done?"

"By ill-chance he may have done – possibly no more than that."

"And so?" Honor breathed.

"And so," Arnot took her up, "though confrontation could be a bad mistake, at least it is bold, and if you play your part and are convincing enough, it could succeed. Better, anyway, than having him go on publicly wondering, gossiping, spreading ideas."

"But supposing I do know him; did meet him in Sydney?"

Arnot threw her an appraising glance. "If you had *met*, I think he wouldn't be wondering aloud; he would be sure. And even if you do know him, must you admit it?"

"N – no. But if he challenges *me* with, say, a time or a place when he saw me with Piers, what then?"

"Why, then you act – with all you have."

"You mean," Honor prompted slowly, feeling a

little sick, dreading his answer, "that you suggest I –
lie?"

She saw the tawny eyes snap in anger. "Don't put
words I haven't used into my mouth," he retorted. "I
said 'act', and 'act' means that you ad lib. You play
it by ear. You finesse. I'd have expected your feminine
nous might know how."

"But if he challenges me outright, what can I say on
the spur of the moment, without a clue as to how
much or how little he knows?"

"I'm sorry, but I must leave that to you."

Honor looked down at her hands, locked in her lap.
"And I'm sorry too. But I can't meet this man. I can't
handle it. I can't – stare him out as you suggest. No –"

"You'd prefer he should be left to his guesswork?
Remember, he has only to mention you in connection
with Piers to a third person, and the talk starts up.
Which, apart from anything else, could put *you* in a
very false position, I'd have thought."

"That's my problem, don't you think, Mr Lord?"
Honor retorted.

"Nonsense!" he snapped. "You haven't *got* a problem, solo. It's all of a piece with mine – that of saving
my mother and Ysanne pain and mortification they
needn't suffer. And may I remind you that you gave
me your word you would go along with me all the way
in this?"

"I only promised to say or do nothing that would
cause them embarrassment."

Arnot exploded, "Tch! – So much negative hair-
splitting! Then you refuse to face Bonner and hear
what he has to say?"

Stung by his doubt of her good faith, Honor hesitated. "I'd – rather not," she said.

"Yet you might agree if I assured you that, once you had made your denial good and strong, the same danger from Bonner couldn't arise again?"

Honor frowned. "I don't understand? How could you ensure that?"

"Never mind. That's my responsibility. Leave it to me." He stood up, as if taking the issue as settled. "And so I may look to see you at La Voile on Sunday after all?"

"I suppose so."

"Good. I'll make things as easy for you as possible," he promised, leaving Honor to wonder bleakly whether she had ever hoped this second clash of wills between them would end in any other way. His steel against hers, she was no match for him. She argued only from the weakness of her personal scruples; he, from the strength of his conviction that the need justified the means. And he would always win.

As it happened, Dorice was not to be one of the party on Sunday night. The previous day she lost her voice in a bout of laryngitis and Adam, called in professionally, prescribed bed and no talking until her temperature dropped.

"A good job Adam·can take you over to La Voile," was the last thing he allowed her to say to Honor. After that it was to be pad and pencil for the next day or two.

"Will she be all right, left alone tonight?" Honor worried on Sunday.

"Oh yes. She's only running a couple of degrees above normal and I'll look in to give her a sedative before we leave. That will put her to sleep, and it's ten to one she won't hear a sound when I bring you back," Adam promised.

Since coming to Grand'terre, Honor had managed to resist most of the temptations of the French dress-shops and the exotic silks on offer in the bazaars. She had succumbed extravagantly only once – to a figure-fitting scarlet dress, severely high-necked in the Chinese fashion and with a daring cheong-sam slit to its skirt.

Deciding to give it its first airing on Sunday's occasion, with a whim to look different from her daytime image, she added a jangle of bazaar-bought silver bracelets, and piled her hair high in loose whorls. The scarlet of the dress seemed to need a heavy cream make-up over her natural flush and tan; a pencil for her brows; a touch of eyeshadow for her lids, mascara for the sweep of her fair lashes – and she was an Honor Troy whom her mirror hardly recognized.

She stared at herself, remembering Arnot's savage challenge to her reflection in another mirror. *Dimension. Shape. Attractions* – persuading her that she had a right to them. But persuading her in cold blood, for his own purposes, not hers. Tonight too he had only one use for her – the confounding of the man Bonner, who might have the power to bring the whole card-castle of their pact crashing down. Why did she allow Arnot to manoeuvre her so? She wished she could deny that, in her heart, she knew . . .

She had the first taste of the effect of her revolt

from the everyday from Adam's long survey of her before he started the car.

Half-turned to her, his arm along the back of her seat, "M'm, exotic," he murmured. "May one ask – a permanent switch from the starched white coat and the dispensary stocksheet? Or a scene laid on just for tonight?"

Self-consciously she smoothed the tight skirt over her knees. "Just for tonight. Don't you approve?" she asked.

Adam shaped his lips for a wolf-whistle. "What man wouldn't?" was his comment. "Not that the pony-tail hairdo and the clinical starch aren't all right by me."

Honor smiled. "By me too. I'm much more at ease in daytime gear."

"But you thought the glamour would 'make a nice change' – as landladies say when they offer you mince with gravy, instead of mince with gravy and snippets of toast?"

"Exactly." They laughed together in easy companionship, and as Adam drove off, Honor found herself thinking, *At least he accepts me without complications* – only to catch, in a brief look he threw her in answer to a glance at his profile, something which disturbed her – a new male awareness of her which she had never seen in his eyes before.

She put the thought from her, hoping she was wrong. Between her and Adam nothing like that must happen. They were professional colleagues, and by that reason alone it wouldn't do. Besides, she had known what it was to love, and nothing of the feeling she had had for Piers stirred in her for Adam.

Because, against all reason, she was on the brink of expending it elsewhere? But she jerked away from that thought as violently as from the other.

At La Voile her doubts as to whether she might have committed the social sin of overdressing for "a small party" were dispelled.

Mrs. Lord was regally patrician in a glittering silver gown; Ysanne was wearing a culotte suit in bizarre shades of peacock, and the male guests had taken to styles and colours which, only a year or so earlier, they would have scorned as acceptable evening wear.

Mrs. Lord touched Honor's cheek with her finger-tips in greeting.

"My dear, I'm so glad you were able to come." She extended a hand to Adam. "Dr. Page too. Tell me, how is poor Dorice? Will she be all right soon? Had she not better come home to convalesce?"

The guests gathered in the long drawing-room for drinks before dinner, the older people in one group, the younger in another with Ysanne as its nucleus.

She made introductions carelessly. "Sue – you know Claude? But of course you do!" "Pelham, meet Honor Troy. Yes, she is new, Dorice's housemate, and very, very earnest. And don't say to her, 'Where have you been all my young life', because she has brought her own young man along, and he is looking daggers at you from over there!" – tilting her head towards Adam, talking to another man.

Honor, nervous lest anyone should forestall Arnot in making the introduction she dreaded, was thankful when he joined their group, drawing her out of it.

They stood apart together. He indicated her empty glass, but did not press her when she did not want it exchanged. He said quietly, "Bonner just arrived – over there. Bow-tie, maroon jacket. No –" as she started and looked in the direction of his slight nod. "Later will do. After dinner. Mother is about to make a move." His hand beneath her elbow, they followed the people leaving the room.

Between making conversation with her dinner partner and listening to the general talk, she glanced covertly at Noel Bonner, relieved to confirm that she had never seen him before to her knowledge. That was something at least, she thought as she noted his distant placing from her at the table, wondering how far that was a chance placing by their hostess, how much Arnot's doing, keeping them apart until it suited him that they should meet.

The meal had reached the dessert stage when the maid Molla, who had left the room after waiting at table, returned to speak quietly to Mrs. Lord.

"Oh dear. What a pity!" Mrs. Lord said aloud, catching the attention of Adam Page a few seats away. "The telephone for you, Dr. Page. Molla will show you where it is, unless she can take a message?"

"Tch! This would happen. Thank you, no, I must take it." He went out with Molla, to return as Mrs. Lord was giving the signal to leave the table.

"I'm so sorry," he apologised. "It's an emergency case I must attend."

"Must you?"

"I'm afraid so." He looked round for Honor, finding her at his side.

"You needn't come with me," he told her, taking her aside to add, "It's that chap I sent for a tooth extraction this morning. His wife is frightened by the amount of haemorrhage still, so I'll have to plug the jaw and give him an antibiotic. But he lives twenty kilometres the other side of the city, so I could be rather late collecting you to take you home."

"If I came with you, you could drop me," Honor suggested.

He shook his head. "Not fair to our hostess or to you. Besides, the plant is way off my route and I want to travel fast."

As Arnot approached to ask "What's the problem?" and to assure Adam that he himself would see Honor home, she watched her faint chance of postponing her ordeal recede. There was no escaping it. Arnot didn't mean that she should.

It was upon her soon after the man came back into the drawing-room. Ysanne began to urge her cronies on to the patio to dance to a radiogram, and Arnot brought Noel Bonner over to Honor.

"Meet a colleague on my sales staff, will you, Honor," he said easily. "Noel Bonner. You have a common bond – he knows Sydney well, from making business trips there. Miss Troy, Noel – you haven't met her, have you?"

Honor offered her hand, saying "How d'you do?" Noel Bonner answered Arnot's question slowly. "N – no. That is, I'm none too sure about that. You remember – I did mention to you that I thought I had seen her somewhere over yonder on my last trip?"

Arnot frowned slightly, as if in search of an unimportant memory. "Oh – yes," he agreed. "But as I recall, you said you had met her with Piers Sabre, didn't you?" He turned casually to Honor. "Piers – my cousin, you know; Ysanne's ex-fiancé?"

She nodded. "Yes, of course –" as the other man disclaimed, "I didn't say 'met'. I only thought I had seen you with Sabre," he told Honor. "And he *was* in Australia at that time."

"Australia being a continent and Sydney quite a city," Arnot commented drily. "It'd be something of a coincidence if –"

He broke off at Bonner's sharp crack of finger and thumb. "Got it!" he exclaimed, sending Honor's heart plunging. "I know where now. True, you didn't see me, nor did Piers, I think. But – at the Loosebox? You know – the nightclub in Madrigal Street? You and Piers were going in as I was leaving. Do you remember the night I could mean? You were there?"

Honor looked straight at him. Beside her she could feel Arnot's listening intensity as almost a physical thing. She drew a long breath, deep as a sigh. She said, "I'm sorry, you must be mistaken. I know the place you mean, the Loosebox Club. But I've never been inside it in my life."

It was, though only by a hair's breadth, the truth, and she could almost have shed tears of relief that she had been able to tell it.

In a daze she heard the gratifying doubt in Noel Bonner's, "No? I could have sworn – Oh well, my mistake. Sorry –" Then, before he had the chance to question her further, Arnot's hand, hard on her arm, was moving her on and away.

71

"Care to dance?" he asked, and when, dumb with relief, she did not reply, he led her out on to the patio and into the rhythm of the dance that was going on.

At the end of it he let her go to another partner and made no opening for seeing her again until people were beginning to leave. Then, after she had thanked Mrs. Lord and was saying good night to Ysanne, he signalled to her that she should join him outside.

Ysanne's parting smile was sweet. "Oh, of course," she commiserated. "You've been abandoned to Arnot's charity, haven't you? You should choose your escort better another time. But you'll be quite safe with Arnot. On principle he doesn't poach on other men's preserves!"

In the car Arnot talked after-party commonplaces for a while. Then he said, "I must congratulate you on your flair in a crisis. When it came to the crunch you said your piece without the flicker of an eyelash."

Honor said, "I wasn't speaking a piece. I was telling the truth, such as it was. Piers Sabre had never taken me into that Club."

Arnot glanced at her. "What do you mean – 'such as it was'?"

"Well –" she hesitated, "there was one evening when he suggested trying it. But from the outside he didn't care for the look of it, so we didn't go in."

"I see. So, though Bonner may indeed have seen you and thought you were on your way in, you were able to give him the lie with a clear conscience?"

"So far. But it was only a half-truth, and –"

"And that troubles you?"

"It's beginning to," she admitted.

"Even though it satisfied Bonner, and it couldn't matter an iota to him, one way or the other? Also the chance that he may have been mistaken about the whole scene. Some other man than Piers. Some other girl."

"He probably wasn't."

"I agree, but with the chance *just* there, I'd say it could acquit you of any guilt over your half-lie. Meanwhile, don't you consider you owed even more conscience to your given word to me that you'd do nothing to force a showdown here about your affair with Piers?" Arnot paused to glance her way again. "Or are you thinking the devil can always make a good case for himself? You're inclined to judge my whole character on my methods of shielding innocent people from pain?"

Honor shook her head. "I – don't know you well enough to judge you."

"No? Yet on the same short acquaintance I've managed to form some opinions of *you*!"

"Judgments can be a good deal more harsh than opinions, and we were talking about judgments," she reminded him.

He agreed blandly, "As you say. Opinions may adjust; judgements are irrevocable. Or are they always? Remind me, won't you, to tell you when I change mine with regard to you?"

At that point, suspecting him of an irony which she knew she was at a loss to answer in the same vein, Honor was thankful to realise they had arrived at the bungalow. Arnot cut the engine and got out of the car with her.

"Thank you for seeing me home," she said formally, and offered him her hand.

He took it, held it as he looked down at her, then drew her closer and kissed her lips.

Though she felt her whole body quiver to the unexpected intimacy of his touch, she allowed her own mouth to give him no response. "Don't, please –" she protested.

By the light of the porch-lantern she saw his expression harden slightly. "Not even as an underlining to my thanks for your co-operation tonight?" he queried.

"You've already congratulated me on that."

"Nor in lieu of a similar tribute Page might have made you, by way of thanking you for his evening? You'd have accepted that with more grace?"

She flushed. "Only if he meant it –" But before she could add the three words she intended – "merely as that" – Arnot flashed savagely,

"– As you judge *I* didn't mean it . . . couldn't, with the expertise which your experience – with Piers for one – has the right to expect? Well, fair enough – you're entitled to your own comparisons. But let's be quite clear. I'm not in competition with either your past or your present. I merely need you as a confederate in a project that means a good deal to me. That's all. *All!* And when I apologise for telling you so, I'll apologise for – *not meaning* this either! "

"This" was the cupping of his hands about her face, a straining tilt of her head and a studied, deliberatly bruising kiss as cruel in intent as his first had been lightly exploratory. She hadn't to break free; he almost

74

thrust her from him. But he waited until she had turned away and used her key – as if, after *that*! he still owed her the common courtesy of seeing her safely indoors!

CHAPTER V

It seemed to Honor that that night's climax put a kind of fog between herself and her future relations with Arnot.

When she tried to think clearly and logically about the unprovoked violence of his parting from her, she could not. For there *was* no logic to a rancour mixed with hurt bewilderment and, even more bafflingly, with a longing to experience the bittersweet of the scene again. She simply did not know what had turned him from suavity to asperity and to . . . assault. For, however politely he might have meant his first kiss, his second had been his explosive rejection of her, except insofar as their uneasy pact went. He had no intention of apologising for it. He had said so. But if he neither apologised nor explained, where did they go from here?

She could not refuse to meet him, nor decline to visit La Voile again. Dorice, eager to share its hospitality with her, would want to know why. And what reason could she give? No, whatever overtures were to be made, they must come from Arnot. In the meanwhile she lived in some dread of Dorice's next invitation to La Voile, not guessing, until Dorice suggested they spend the coming week-end at her home, how readily she would snatch at the chance to confront Arnot with a question which had no hazy nimbus of fog to it; one to which she meant to get his plain yes or no.

The urgency had arisen from a casual remark Dorice made after Honor, not without misgivings, had accepted the invitation. With no idea of the import to Honor of the news, Dorice said, "A bit of a crisis on Arnot's hands just now, I gather from Tante Rachel. Sales manager Helman blowing his top; Arnot doing his "Who is the boss around here?" stuff. All because, just as Helman had scheduled the salesmen's territories and itineraries for the season, Arnot stepped in, told Helman he must scrub all his careful graphs with regard to one of the export men, Bonner, as Bonner, on Arnot's orders, wouldn't be available. He had taken yesterday's New Zealand flight out."

Honor had to suppress a gasp. As casually as she could, she queried, "Would that be a man named Noel Bonner, whom I met at Mrs. Lord's party, the night you couldn't go?"

Dorice nodded. "The very same. He comes from New Zealand, I think."

"But did Arnot mean he had dismissed him – or what?"

"Could be, I suppose. Tante Rachel only reported the wrangle. No details, and I wasn't very interested. Bonner has a habit of drinking too much, and when he's in his cups he tattles gossip like a fishwife. So if Arnot has got rid of him, he'll be no great loss," Dorice concluded.

But he still had the right to ordinary justice, thought Honor indignantly, remembering Arnot's hint that if she confronted Bonner successfully, he would see that

77

she wasn't troubled again. Had he meant even then to dismiss the man before he could have second thoughts about her and Piers? The very notion was sickening, and she knew she would not rest until she learned the truth of just how far in ruthlessness Arnot was prepared to go, in order to save Ysanne Faudron distress.

It meant she must force some opportunity to speak to him alone when she and Dorice went over to La Voile. It wasn't likely that after their last encounter, he would make that easy, and in fact it was Mrs. Lord who brought the chance about.

Grand'terre-born and proud of her heritage, she was concerned to hear that as yet Honor had had little time for exploring the island or learning much about its age-old history and customs. What was more, born hostess that she was, she saw it as her duty to fill any guest's leisure as pleasurably as she could.

At dinner on the first evening of the girls' week-end she took Dorice to task. "Port Maré! The beaches! The Yacht Club! What else beyond this sorry triangle have you shared with Honor so far? Ah, as I thought, very little. You young people gravitate from one set of bright lights to the other and back again – missing so much on the way." Turning from Dorice to Arnot across the table, "Now what can we show Honor of the real Grand'terre in these few hours that we have her under our roof? City shops, Club bars, beaches noisome with transistor radios – these she can find anywhere. The beauty of Grand'terre, nowhere else in the world!"

Arnot's smile was affectionately indulgent. "In English, mother mine, 'noisome' means smelly; isn't

78

'raucous' the word you want?" he queried.

She shrugged. "If you say so, though to my ears 'noisome' means better what *I* mean. And you haven't answered my question – how best can we entertain Honor while she is with us this week-end?" Abandoning him, she brought her attention back to Honor. "You, my dear, what have you seen of, for example, our wild West Coast, or the rain forests, or the Kanaka villages, or even the mangrove swamps?"

"Well, only as much as I've seen on one or two up-country medical visits I've made with Dr. Page," Honor admitted.

"Oh – you travel with him?" Mrs. Lord sounded surprised.

"Professionally. When he attends Kanaka women or children," Honor told her.

"Ah yes – the old taboo by which even a doctor may not be trusted alone with a woman," Mrs. Lord agreed, and then settled pleasurably to her plans. Her imperious glance round the table took in Arnot, Ysanne and Dorice as well as Honor. "Tomorrow then," she announced, "we shall all make a day of picnic along the coast. Perhaps as far as Chephien; perhaps beyond, to Baie Liane. Arnot? What do you say?"

He stirred his coffee. "That I happen to be a working man, Mother, and that you can't spring 'a day of picnic' on me just like that," he replied.

She scowled at him. "Ah, you are difficult. But you will come," she said complacently. "Dorice – you too? And Ysanne?"

Dorice said, "Sorry, I'm riding, Tante Rachel."

Ysanne said plaintively, "Oh dear, must I, Tante

79

Rachel? Do you really want me? Because I *had* promised the Rozels that I would crew for them tomorrow. Though of course, if –?"

Mrs. Lord shook her head at the three of them. "So – reluctant wedding-guests, all of you? Very well. I will excuse you girls, but as Honor and I must have a chauffeur, I shall expect you, Arnot, to arrange to accompany us. Cook shall prepare us a luncheon hamper, and we shall be away for the whole day. It will, after all, be Saturday, and you can spare our guest that, I feel sure."

Arnot pushed aside his cup and rose. "Then you must excuse me now." As he passed her chair he laid a hand upon her shoulder. "Did anyone ever have the moral courage to say no to you, Mother?" he chaffed her.

She looked up at him, her fine eyes wide. "Oh yes," she said.

"I can't believe it! Who?"

"Your father –"

"And what happened?"

"I admired his spirit so much that I married him – Honor, my dear, I am sure that if you will go with Arnot to his study, he will show you on the wall-map he keeps there just where our little trip will take us."

Honor half-rose, glancing at Arnot, who nodded coolly. "If you must be briefed, now is as good as any other time. Will you come?" he said.

In his study he stood behind her at the wall-map of the long cigar-shape of the island, his forefinger pointing from over her shoulder at the western coastline.

"Port Maré – here. Here are we." The finger travelled. "Chephien – my mother's objective – inland here. Back to the coast, Liane here. The coral reef in view most of the way. Flatter and less picturesque than the east coast, but less explored and exploited by that reason –" His tone, making the recital, had the impersonality of an official guide, draining his descriptions of warmth, underlining the distance he had put between himself and her, and daunting her resolve to ask the question which had to be put ... and answered while they were alone.

He was using a pencil now to trace the inland road they would take across the savannah, with the flat coastal plain to their left, the mountain chain to their right. At one point the pencil paused and stabbed a cross on the map. "Here, I've no doubt, my mother means you to see one of our natural curiosities – in this form, it's unique to Grand'terre, and this is one of the spots where it is to be found," he said.

"Oh? What is it?" Honor asked.

He shook his head. "No, I think I'll leave that scene to her. Before now I've heard her draw a certain moral from it, and I'd hate to steal her thunder." With which he flicked the pencil back on to his desk and Honor realised the moment she dreaded had come.

She turned to face him. "There's something I want to ask you," she said. "You may consider it's none of my business, but I think it is."

"If it isn't," he returned, "you can be very sure I'll tell you so. Well?"

"It's about Mr. Bonner."

"What about Bonner?"

"Well, Dorice happened to mention that he has left

the island suddenly, and that you sent him away."

"And if I did, is that any concern of yours?"

"Well, isn't it?" she countered. "I know you told me you would see to it that I shouldn't have to fear meeting him again. But I never dreamed you would go quite so far in injustice, for the risk of anything else he might remember or talk of about me."

"So far? How far?"

"Why, to dispense with him, as Dorice says you have done."

"If you mean 'sack', why not say so? Meanwhile, perhaps Dorice should get her facts right before she passes them on to outsiders whom they don't concern."

Though Honor flinched at the ice in his tone, her heart leaped to the hope which his words gave her.

"Then you didn't –?" she began lamely.

"Wave Bonner off on the first available New Zealand flight? Oh, but I did!" As Arnot leaned easily against the edge of the desk and folded his arms Honor sensed that in the space of minutes, mastery of the situation had passed to him. She, his accuser of bad faith, was now in the dock; he had sloughed the defensive like a skin.

Their eyes met, his now tolerant of her discomfiture; almost – could she believe it? – amused as, on an edge of irony which he must know would cut, he said, "I may take it, I imagine, that I'm at liberty to give one of my own employees prolonged leave of absence to suit his convenience and my own? Or not?"

She felt trapped, yet at the same time, so flooded with relief that she could afford humility. "Won't you explain?" she begged. "You must know I took what

Dorice told me at its face value? That I didn't understand —?"

"And still chose to condemn me unheard?" But there was now no asperity in his tone as he continued, "All right — here's as much as you need to understand. In a few weeks' time, Bonner was due for his biennial long home-leave. I decided to advance its date; he was only too willing to take it, as his mother is ill. He booked his flight and departed, and do you consider you've any legitimate quarrel with that?"

Honor bit her lip. "Of course not. But when I remembered you had told me he wouldn't trouble me again, I thought —"

"Exactly what you thought was written all over you. You don't need to spell it out," he cut in. "But as long as it has cleared the air?"

"Yes. Thank you." As there seemed no more to say, she turned away, only to halt at his question,

"Don't you want to know how long Bonner's leave is to be? In fact, he had some due to him, so it'll be all of six months."

She looked at him, puzzled. Then she said slowly, "I see. You mean that when he does come back, there won't be — any problem? That I shall have gone myself?"

"Well, won't you? You've been here several weeks already, and when I asked you whether you'd be taking up your option to leave, you left me in no doubt of your answer," he reminded her.

Wanting to be rid of her! Counting the very days until she ceased to hold any threat to Ysanne Faudron's peace of mind! But seeing he was waiting for her reply, she said, "Yes, I remember. And six months from now will more than cover that, won't it?"

"By my calculations —"

As she moved again towards the door, he followed her to open it, adding, "In the circumstances, I daresay you see Mother's determination to show you Grand'terre as so much waste of time?"

"Not at all. I'm very grateful to her for wanting to."

"Well at any rate, under her chaperonage tomorrow, you shouldn't find yourself in danger of any further assault from me, should you?" he remarked.

But from the calculated irony of that she took refuge in merely standing there, waiting for him to open the door.

She woke to dread of a day which should have been all pleasure. But Mrs. Lord's anticipation of her "day of picnic" was so infectious that it was difficult to resist her enthusiasm.

After watching the ample picnic hamper taken aboard, she insisted that Honor sit beside Arnot, herself taking the back seat where, her lorgnettes at the ready as she pored over the large-scale map on her lap, she plied Arnot with navigational directions which he took in good part, but which he obviously did not need.

As they drove up-country it would have been churlish to grudge its scenic beauty all the admiration it deserved. Somehow personal problems were faded out while the tawny savannahs, the blue-shadowed mountains, the primitive villages and the cloudless arc of the sky were there to be revelled in and enjoyed to the full.

The dry soil of the savannahs encouraged little

growth but bamboo and stunted scrub and sturdy, gnarled niaouli trees, their flowers dangling like catkins, the scent of their foliage as sickly-sweet as honeysuckle. But further west, where sheltered valleys were watered by countless small rivers running down to the coast there was a flourish of blackwoods and feathery casuarinas and areca palm, and wherever there was water there were groups of mud-walled, reed-thatched beehive little houses, where people idled in the sun, and children ran out to wave and call greetings to the passing car.

Chephien, Mrs. Lord's objective, was one such lush district, its huddle of houses boasting a village-shop and a central open square where the weekly stores and mail-van was parked, surrounded by eager clients, clamouring for service and for as much news as the mail-man could give them of their relatives and friends all the way out from Port Maré.

Chephien's irrigating water was a long creek, where little boats rocked gently and fishing-nets were spread on the banks. Arnot turned the car up-stream from the village and halted for their picnic meal in a palm-shaded grove a few kilometres further inland. They unpacked the hamper and set out the food; Arnot poured wine and Mrs. Lord promised Honor,

"Afterwards, Arnot shall show you something we brought you here to see. It is to be found hereabouts; he knows where –" She broke off, lifting her head to listen. "Ah, and there is something else of the real Grand'terre for you to hear – That bird-call. You hear it now? It *is* the kagu, isn't it?" she appealed to Arnot.

He nodded. Honor, listening, heard only the plain-

85

tive "Ow-Ow" yelp of a puppy from the heart of the woodland behind their grove. "That's not a bird?" she queried, mystified.

Mrs. Lord chuckled. "You wouldn't think so, would you? But it is indeed our poor kagu, whom you may see on our postage stamps. Long ago, when he had to fear no hunters, he lost the power to fly, and the story goes that when men came to Grand'terre and tracked him for food, he learned to imitate the baying of their dogs. But he didn't deceive the hounds. He was hunted all the same, and now there are very few of him left."

"Is he ever seen?" asked Honor.

"Very seldom in his wild state, though there is a pair in the botanical gardens in Port Maré. He is very protective of his mate, as every good husband should be. Isn't that true, Arnot?"

"Of the model husband, or of the kagu?" he parried.

"Of both, as you know very well," his mother retorted. "However they may deny it, all women need a man to lean upon, and even our kagu, going through his sad little play of pretending to be a dog, is doing his best to prove his worth. However, I am glad Honor has heard him today. For in all the time she is still here with us, she might not hear him again. And now, are we ready to eat? Arnot, pass Honor one of those little tubs of chicken in aspic. Yes, and the green salad. . . . Have you everything you want, my dear? Then let us drink – What do you suggest that we drink to, Arnot?"

"Why not to the survival of the kagu?"

Mrs. Lord nodded sadly. "Alas, poor kagu! But no, I think we will include him in a toast to the lasting chivalry of men, without which we women would be in poor trim indeed. Come—!"

Their glasses were lifted in the little ceremony she demanded, then she presided at the meal spread on the grass as graciously as at her own table. She related anecdotes and island customs for Honor's hearing, now and then appealing to Arnot for detail; making her small party 'go' as smoothly as if it were a banquet.

Honor, to her surprise, found her tension giving way to an ease with Arnot which she had never known before. Today he was relaxed, urbane, solicitous – the man she supposed his friends knew and cared about, rather than the one who had seen fit to prejudge *her* without cause. This, she supposed, was the Arnot Ysanne knew; the man to whom she had been able to turn for shelter when Piers had let her down. Ysanne had some quality of appeal to his chivalry which she herself had not. But today, in his mother's company, no one would have guessed that any cross-currents of strain ran between them. And when, an hour later, Mrs. Lord dismissed them both to go in search of the curiosity Honor had been brought to see, his hand, now on her shoulder, now taking hers to guide her over the rough places, was companionable, protective, easy.

Their objective was a stream which had gouged a narrow bed for itself between rock. Its banks were steeply treacherous, needing Arnot's guiding of Honor's footholds, step by step. At last they were at stream level where, after a short search, Arnot thrust aside a tangle of thorn and fern to reveal a scatter of rocks of all sizes, each deeply incised by what could only be man-engraved patterns – triangles, broken squares, eyes, raying suns, rosettes, petalled flowers.

"Oh –!" Honor knelt heedlessly in the scrub to trace their lines with her fingers. "They're *drawings!*" she breathed. "How old are they? Who did them?"

Arnot said, "They're known as petroglyphs, and in this form they're unique to Grand'terre. For the rest, there's argument as to their age or whether the original men on the island had the tools to work on rock as hard as this. But they worked this same stone into axes and missiles, so why not carving-instruments too? As to what they mean, they could be an alphabet or a secret code or mere doodles to pass the time. And for them there must have been all the time in the world."

"That's what they look like, "Honor agreed, "just idle doodling. Because they aren't even finished. Look, here's a walking-stick head, and here's part of a dagger . . . or is it supposed to be a bird in flight? But oh!" enthusiastically she cleared a large rock of its loose dust – "here *is* a complete design, a real flower! Are they found anywhere else in the island? Or only just here?"

"In a few other places, not many," Arnot told her. "The powers that be have had the taste to leave them where they are to be found, and those of us who are in the know are jealous enough of them only to let a chosen few into the secret of their whereabouts."

Honor sat back on her heels, making a business of dusting down her skirt. "Well, thank you for showing them to me," she said.

"You should thank Mother for sensing that you

would appreciate them. Well, if you've seen enough –?" He offered her a hand to pull her to her feet, accepted her help in replacing the curtain of greenery over and about the engravings, and directed her in the steep return climb up the bank.

To Honor's eager enthusiasm over the petroglyphs Mrs. Lord returned a pleased, "So Arnot found them for you, and you are glad to have seen them? Good. That makes you one of us, and one of the few people, I hope, to whom I can tell my own idea of what they mean, without fear of being laughed at."

"As if," Arnot murmured, as he began to repack their picnic gear into the car, "as if, Mother, you ever feared anyone's laughing at you, or as if anyone ever dared to try it on!"

"Ah, you! You make fun of your poor Maman!" With a truly Gallic shrug she dismissed him as she confided to Honor, "Now *I* think they were love-letters. No? You don't agree?"

"Er – love – letters?" Honor doubted, playing for time.

"Yes, why not? When I was young we used to seal our *billets-doux* with secret codes, and stone was all the writing-paper these people had. And so an arrow could mean 'I am coming to you', a sinuous curve, 'You are lovely', a flower – Why, sometimes when I cannot sleep, I devise meanings for them all –"

"And never ask yourself why the recipients left them about so carelessly, instead of tying them up with pink ribbon and hiding them in a corner of their cave?" Arnot teased.

But his mother was ready for that with her own brand of logic. "Never," she declared loftily. "If only because, as you should know very well, Arnot, that in those days there would have *been* no pink ribbon!" But as the other two laughed, her fine face shadowed. "All the same," she added, "you should leave an old woman her dreams. To me a rosette carved deep into stone means only one thing: that someone, long ago, knew that marriage without love is just so much bare rock. So he gave it love as well, in the only way he knew, by carving a flower on it with all the trouble and care that marriage needs to keep it sweet." Then briskly she was on her feet, making plans for the rest of the outing. "Now we shall go back by way of the coast. Honor may like to swim at Baie Liane. I shall rest. Arnot, what are we waiting for?"

As soon as they touched the coast road the line of the coral reef was continually in view, a luminous barrier between an indigo sea and the burnished calm of the inshore lagoon. Little dunes, spiky with marram grass, sloped down from the road, palms grew almost to the water's edge. Baie Liane was a silver-sanded crescent bitten out of the land, palm-shaded, deserted and immensely silent but for the gentle lip-lip murmur of the tideless lagoon water caressing the shore.

Mrs. Lord settled under an umbrella palm. Arnot changed first in the car and was already swimming strongly far out when Honor had slipped out of the play-dress she had worn over her two-piece swim suit and went to kick her way through the shallows into deeper water.

She idled, trod water, floated, eyes closed to the glare of the sun, and experimented with some porpoise dives and turns. Arnot came back, suggesting a leisurely crawl round the jut of dunes which bounded their bay from its neighbour. "If you can't make it, say so," he told her. "But if you can manage it, you can rest on shore before we go back."

She was gratified to show that she could manage it easily, and she was only a few strokes behind him when, round the bluff, he found shallow water and stood up. But when she made to do likewise pain stabbed through the ball of her left foot, and, gasping, she fell on all fours, her head bent to hide the tears of shock which had sprung to her eyes.

Mistily she was aware of Arnot's striding back to her, attempting to lift her, but desisting when she shook her head. "It's my foot. I – can't stand," she faltered.

He knelt to turn her into a sitting position, his hands on her shoulders. "It's not cramp?"

"No. My left foot. Something sticking into it, I think. Something . . . sharp."

"Let me see." His touch was probing but gentle. "Ah – !" He cradled her foot. "You've picked up a sea-urchin's spine, and your standing just now has driven it further. It's got to come out – and fast. Sea-urchins are dirty feeders."

She nodded weak agreement.

"It's going to hurt," he warned.

"All right." She felt him probe again, as at a colossal thorn, braced herself to the pain, but fell back against the sand as the wrench came and she felt the

91

slow trickle of blood down her foot.

She felt sick, prayed she needn't be so in shaming fact, and felt Arnot's arms about her, sitting her up, then thrusting her head down to her knees.

The black nausea passed. Foolishly smiling with relief, she lifted her head, her hand colliding with his as they both made to brush teardrops from her cheek.

"You've some dangerous bathing around these parts," she said shakily.

He was scooping water to staunch the blood which still trickled from the wound. "And you should know better than to swim without sandals around these parts. If I'd seen you barefoot, you wouldn't have gone in," he retorted.

"I know. Dorice warned me, but I forgot to bring sandals with me. I always do wear them."

"I should think so. There's always loose coral battered from the reef, and though it's a million to one chance that a sea-urchin would spear you or you would pick up a shed spine, you can't be too careful." He sat back. "All right now?" he asked.

"Yes, thank you."

"Evidently nerves of steel. Ysanne, for one, would have had hysterics," he commented.

"She's probably more highly-strung than I am."

"And Latin to her fingertips. Mixed Corsican and Italian. Which makes her the bundle of emotions she is, though with careful handling, she can be gratifyingly flexible. Whereas you—"

He paused, as if expecting Honor's question, but when she was silent, he went on, "Whereas I'd judge you to be as much the product of your own cool, detached English stock as Ysanne is of hers. By comparison with her temperament as, say, marble is to plasticine."

"And as workable material, I suppose you prefer plasticine?" Honor couldn't resist that cut at the persuasion he had used on her, and from the swift shrewd glance he threw her, she realised he had taken the point.

"Let's say, shall we," he offered, "that I've always thought marble must be pretty cussed stuff to work on, and that a man does like to see results?" Then he was standing, dismissing the subject. "If you're ready, shall we be making a move?" he said.

Doubtfully Honor measured the distance from the shallow to her estimate of the deeper water. "If you'll help me out," she said.

He stared. "*Out?*"

"To where I can swim."

"Swim?" he echoed again. "You're not swimming back with that foot!"

"How, then?"

"This way, of course. Across the dunes to where we left the car and where you'll need some first aid. I never travel without the necessary gear."

"But how?"

"How? So —" With which he bent, scooped her into his arms; straightened, balancing her weight and set out upshore at an easy, long-paced stride.

On the half-kilometre or so of distance through the shifting sand of the dunes, he spoke only once. That was when he looked down into her face, close against his shoulder, and remarked cryptically, "All that steel, and there's no weight to you at all!" But on that same short journey something magical happened to Honor. In his arms, if only by reason of her accident, she had the right to lean against him with softness and with purpose, for all the world as if, like lovers, they both wanted it this way – the encircling hold, the quickened heartbeats, the physical nearness which, shared with him might have been a sweet danger, but of which only she was achingly aware.

Until now her mind had given this turmoil other names – affronted pride, pique, challenge. But now she knew it for what it was – her need to stand well with the man she loved; to be seen to have worth and value and a warmth of spirit which passionately longed for answer, but which would go on loving, even when there was no answer to come.

As there was, and would be, none to hers from Arnot ... though while he was cradling her body closely and tenderly, his care allowed her to pretend, to dream ... for this little while, disarming her defences against him.

Later there would be time enough – all the time in the world – for the cold sanity of the everyday in which they were, at best, uneasy allies. But for the moment *this* was her stolen Now of make-believe.

CHAPTER VI

SANITY returned with Mrs. Lord's concern, with Arnot's deft first aid and with the rest of the week-end, the Sunday of which Honor and Dorice spent alone while Arnot drove Mrs. Lord and Ysanne to a luncheon party with friends. Between Friday's outward journey to La Voile and the drive back on Sunday evening, nothing had happened but a pleasant family week-end, except for Honor, and what had happened to her didn't show.

On the way back Dorice had been driving in silence for some time when, à propos of nothing, she said, "You know, I'm worried about Ysanne."

Honor jerked from her own thoughts. "About Ysanne? Why?" she queried.

"Well, d'you remember that she begged off Tante Rachel's picnic idea because she wanted to crew for the Rozels?"

"Yes, I remember," Honor agreed. "Who are the Rozels?"

"Friends of ours. You haven't met them. A brother and a sister who are mad on sailing. But the odd thing is," Dorice frowned, "that while I was out riding, who should I meet but Clare Rozel, who said that though they had meant to sail yesterday, Paul – that's her brother – had dropped a huge mallet on his foot the day before, Friday, and that he wouldn't be taking their boat out for at least a week. And yet Ysanne –"

"Perhaps they hadn't let her know the trip was off

95

by the time Mrs. Lord suggested the picnic," Honor suggested.

Dorice shook her head. "No, it wasn't that. They didn't need to let her know, because they hadn't asked her to join them. They'd got a boy cousin staying with them, who was going to crew for them. So it never was on for Ysanne. But she still went off in her car on Saturday without saying a word."

"Nor when she came back?"

"Not even when I asked if she had had a good day, and she said yes. *That* was when I'd expected her to say she hadn't been out with Clare and Paul. Instead she let me think she had been, and I don't know why."

"You didn't ask her, or tell her you had seen Clare Rozel?"

"I hardly liked to. Facing someone with a lie they've told takes a bit of crust, don't you find? Besides, she is such a vulnerable little thing that I'd hate to force her to crumple up and admit it, when whatever ploy she'd really been on might be something quite simple and innocent."

"You'd rather worry then as to what she *was* up to?" Honor asked drily, knowing her sympathy was far less with Ysanne than with Dorice's concern about her.

Dorice shrugged. "Somehow one has grown the habit of worrying about Ysanne. Especially since Piers jilted her, and when one knows the standard that Arnot set for her – namely that, though in his eyes she can do no wrong, she mustn't ever risk his suspecting that she might. I suppose that's why we all rally round her like mad. Because we know that if she ever did fall short of his idea of her, he could be merciless. Arnot is like that. He doesn't forgive easily. I doubt if he'll ever forgive Piers, for one," Dorice concluded.

Honor shivered inwardly at this view of the man to whom, unasked, she had given her love. Aloud she said, "But aren't you seeing something sinister which may not be there at all, simply in Ysanne's telling a rather petty lie and not taking it back?"

"Yes. Yes, I suppose so," Dorice agreed. "It's just that there is a French saying about *un ange déchu* – meaning that a fallen idol comes down with a bigger crash than anything else. But of course you're right. I'm simply seeing bogeymen that aren't there. Forget it." But her tone lacked conviction, and a few days later there was a sequel to Ysanne's default which involved them both.

Suddenly, well before the time of the seasonal rains, the hitherto perfect weather broke. Cloud gathered far out to sea and hung unmoving for hours over the lagoons, the bays and the island. The upper slopes of the mountain chain were hidden in mist, and every day, when the clouds could hold no more moisture, the rain came down; straight, relentless rods of it in the windless, brooding calm.

The earlier hours of the days were comparatively dry, and people hurried about their business then, later keeping to their homes. Which was why, on a late afternoon, when a light rain had already begun, Honor and Dorice were surprised by a visit by Ysanne.

She ran in from her car, to be greeted by Dorice's blunt, "What goes? You must be mad to come over in this weather!"

Ysanne shook out her damp hair and threw it back. "It wasn't raining when I came away."

"But you might have known it would. It always does, these nights."

"Yes. Only, you see, I wanted to ask a favour of you."

"A favour? Go ahead," Dorice invited. "Though couldn't you have phoned?"

"No. I had to come over, because I'm on my way to a date, and – well, Tante Rachel thinks I'm spending the evening here with you."

"And one gathers you aren't spending the evening here with us?" Dorice stated flatly.

"Well, I've come here, so I didn't lie. But no – I'm going on. It was just that I wanted to ask you –" Ysanne's glance included Honor – "whether, though the question isn't likely to come up, you would say I was here all the while."

"I see. And this date – it wouldn't, by chance, be the same one you kept on the Saturday you didn't crew for the Rozels?" Dorice pounced.

Ysanne's dark eyes sparked with alarm. "How did you know about that?"

Dorice told her. She bit her lip. "You didn't tell Tante Rachel or – or anyone that I wasn't with Clare and Paul?"

Dorice shrugged. "None of my business, I thought. But if you're asking us to cover up for you, this is. Who is the man?"

Ysanne looked away. "You wouldn't know him," she muttered.

"I might. Try me."

"His name is Germain Trèves."

"Trèves?" Dorice stared. "But he is one of Arnot's copra hands! Ysanne, you *can't*!"

"Why not? He's attractive and exciting, and he says he has been crazy about me for ages without daring to say so. He's *different*!"

"Different? I'll go along with that, all right. He's not one of us, and he's got a – reputation. Ysanne, you simply can't – not after Piers and –" As Dorice paused, Honor wondered with a stab of pain whether she had stopped short of adding – "and now Arnot". But as Dorice paused Ysanne cut in bitterly,

"And Piers was such a prize, such a treasure, wasn't he? Jilting me for that pick-up in Australia and making me the laughing-stock of the whole island! And how do *you* know what it's like for me at La Voile now? *You* got out as soon as you could, leaving me alone with Tante Rachel and Arnot, who is always either in his office or out on the estate. Piers indeed! Just because to *you* he was perfect, you don't expect *me* to have any fun ever again!"

Honor watched Dorice's bright colour darken at the gibe. But she said restrainedly, "As far as I can see, you don't lack for fun. You've a car of your own; Arnot takes you about, and Tante Rachel couldn't be sweeter to you. And she has no real obligations to you. She does employ you, after all."

"Thank you. That's all I wanted!" Ysanne flashed back. "To be reminded that I'm just a Cinderella type, a paid companion, who was, all the same, good enough for your precious twin until –"

This time it was Dorice who cut in. "We'll leave

Piers out of this, if you don't mind," she said tautly. "All I'm saying now is that you are a lot too good for a man like Germain Trèves, and I'm surprised you don't know there's no future with him for a girl like you."

Ysanne pouted. "Pff! Who's bothered about the future? I want some fun now. But all right – *don't* try to understand. I'm sorry I thought you might be friendly enough to help me, if only to make up for the way Piers treated me. It seems I was wrong."

"Yes, well –" Dorice appeared to waver. "Look, where are you meeting Trèves? Where is he taking you?"

"Does it matter?"

"I want to know."

"We're going to the In Place down on the quays. It's a discotheque, and there's a dining-bar."

"It's a dive," snapped Dorice. "However, you are just spending the evening there, that's all?"

"Of course. I'm not proposing to elope with Germain, and I can't afford to be later home than I should be if I'd been here with you, can I?"

"All right, then we'll strike a bargain. I'll agree to cover for you if I must, on condition you don't see Trèves clandestinely again, expecting help from me or from Honor. Is it a deal?"

"That's not fair. You won't even be asked about me!" Ysanne protested.

"Let's hope not. But after tonight you don't see him again without Tante Rachel's knowing. O.K.?"

"Oh, very well." Having got her way, Ysanne's face cleared. She went to the window and looked out. "It's hardly raining yet, so I'll go now. And don't worry, I shan't be late back, and when I go in, all Tante Rachel will say will be, 'And how were Dorice and Honor?' I shall say, 'Fine', and that will be that. Finis," she said pertly, answered Dorice's question to say she wouldn't look in on her way home, and was gone.

Dorice looked diffidently at Honor. "You think I was weak with her, don't you?" she asked.

Honor said, "I'm wondering whether she will keep her promise to you."

"M'm. Remains to be seen. But I had to use some lever on her. You see that?"

"I suppose so, though I wish you hadn't to get involved at all."

"But she had already involved me. You too, indirectly. I couldn't get out without going to the telephone and telling Tante Rachel that Ysanne had lied to her. And somehow, though you wouldn't understand this, not having the same guilt I have towards Ysanne, I do feel I owe her something because of Piers — you know?" Dorice appealed.

You too! Mrs. Lord; Arnot; I by my silence . . . you. All of us cherishing Ysanne Faudron, guarding her from Piers, telling our lies by omission for her — are we all mad? thought Honor in a moment of clarity which she longed to be free to share with Dorice. But all she said aloud was, "May I say I didn't think you were very wise to let Ysanne know you still feel responsible for Piers. It gave her a — a screw to turn on you, as it were."

Dorice laughed shortly. "And her timing was perfect, wasn't it? It got results —" Then she squared her shoulders, as if throwing off a problem. "Oh well —

this time, no consequences, one hopes. And there'd better not be a next time – or else!" She broke off, tilting her head to listen. "Heavens! Hark at that for rain, will you? It's throwing it down!"

It was – as inevitably as, at about the same hour, it had done for nearly a week, bouncing off the stone of the patio, cascading from the roof, making canals of the garden paths. Far out, in the direction of the sea there was thunder, and the accompanying darkness was swiftly that of full night.

Drawing curtains and switching on lamps, Dorice said, "It's often fairly local. Let's hope the worst of it doesn't catch up with Ysanne before she gets to Port Maré." Dorice paused to muse, "Funny, that. The way we've made a habit of hoping this and fearing that for Ysanne, when, on tonight's showing, she has been quietly resenting all of us for various reasons. Arnot, for not dancing attendance on her as often as she'd like; Tante Rachel, for expecting her rights as an employer; me, for getting out on my own and for daring to be Piers' twin. Next thing you know, she'll be working up a grudge against you, young Honor, for utterly no reason at all!"

Though against me she has more reason than for all the rest, thought Honor, assailed again by the guilt of knowledge she must not share. As it was, the only reply she could think of was an easy, "Well, let's hope not." and had just made it when, with the defiant finality of such crises, all the lights went out.

Across the pitch-black room came Dorice's exasperated, "Well, that's *all* it wanted to make a merry evening! I wonder if the power has gone too?"

It had. Groping back from the nearest power switch, she announced, "Guess what? We haven't a candle in the place, and as we're thatched, we mustn't store oil for lamps – *if* we owned an oil-lamp, *which* we don't. So now what?"

Honor laughed. "We twiddle our thumbs in the dark and play 'I Spy'."

"Joke, ha-ha. We could be playing it all night," Dorice grunted. As she went to draw back curtains with some benefit to the darkness in the room, the telephone shrilled and, abandoning the last curtain, she plunged to answer it.

Listening, Honor heard her side of the exchange.

" . . . Yes, speaking," said Dorice. "Yes . . . Oh *no*? Where? . . . As bad as that? Oh yes, we've had it . . . got it still, though by the sound of it, it is giving over. Light and power gone, though. Oh – not with you? Some folks have all the luck. We –"

She broke off, listened in a longer silence to her caller, then said with an odd hesitancy, "Er – yes. Yes, of course. M'm, yes, I'll tell her. She's to wait for you –" and rang off.

Her shadowy figure turned. "That was Arnot," she said flatly. "Their power isn't off, but they've had torrential rain. That bridge over the creek, a kilometre from La Voile, is down, and the road is impassable to cars. He is coming over to take Ysanne back by a détour, and she is to wait until he comes. Well?"

Honor breathed, "Oh *no*! And she isn't here! What can you do? Anything *I* can do –?"

Dorice shook her head. "No. If that low haunt is on the telephone, which I doubt, I could ring, though

103

how do I know she would come back?"

"Oh, surely she must realise the risk?" Honor protested.

"All the same, *I'm* not risking that I might not get her, or that she might refuse. I'm going down to bring her back. It's the only way," Dorice declared.

"But supposing Arnot gets here first?"

Dorice calculated. "I don't think he can. He'll have to make a big détour if he can't use the coast road. No, I can do it, I think. And anyway, I'd rather be *acting*, instead of sitting here, chewing the cud as to whether she'd show up in time or not."

Honor had to let her go, seeing her out to her car by the light of a pocket-torch, then turning back into the house for her own dim vigil.

Her sight adjusting itself, she was able to move about. But as there was nothing she could do without light, she sat by a window, listening to the reluctant cessation of the rain, until the sound of water dripping and pouring came only from the gentle plop-plop from the leaves of the trees and the gushing of runnels towards the drains. In imagination she followed Dorice's journey down to the city quays; Arnot's, by some way she had probably never travelled and so couldn't picture; trying to time them both, praying that Dorice's double trip would be the shorter. Praying? Yes, because Ysanne had culpably involved Dorice in her shabby lie, and if it were found out, Dorice would lose face, if no more, with Arnot too.

Honor's thoughts went off at a sudden tangent. Adam, she suddenly remembered, had two good-battery-powered lamps. The lighting of his bungalow would have failed too, but if he were at home and would lend one of his lamps, to go over and fetch it would be something to do while she waited for the others' return. It wasn't raining at all now.

When there was no answer to her knock at Adam's door, it occurred to her that she might have telephoned first. But the door itself was only on the latch, so she went in, finding her way through the lounge to the kitchen which was identical with their own. She knew Adam's habit of leaving notes for his boy-cook on the kitchen table and, using her torch, she saw there was one. "Back at eight o'clock", Adam had written, and as it was nearly eight now, she decided to wait for a few minutes. Either Adam or his boy should be arriving before long, and for the purpose of borrowing the lamp, either of them would suit her.

In fact she waited for so long that she was on the point of leaving when a clatter and a stamping of boots heralded the arrival of the boy Taju, a small dark figure behind the beam of his own torch, covering his surprise at sight of her with a clamour of apologies for his lateness in getting Mastar's evening meal. The storm . . . the power failure . . . no trolley-bus running. Mastar had invited the ma'am to eat with him? Alas, all there was to eat must be cold –! Honor at last managed to stem the flow by explaining her actual errand, and Taju had just produced the lamp and handed it over when Adam himself arrived.

Honor explained again. "Of course, of course! Anything that's mine is yours," he grinned. "I won't ask you to share a crust with me by lamplight, because when I've eaten, I've got to go straight out again on

105

a locum call. But I'll walk you back first. Here, give me that thing. I'll carry it."

With the lamp in the crook of one arm, he linked Honor closely with the other and matched his step to hers. After the rain, the air was humid, sweet, a potpourri of distilled scents and muted night-sounds. Adam's fingers crept towards Honor's palm, then held her hand. He said nothing. Nor did she. But she sensed he was making an approach, putting a silent question which, though she left her hand in his, she didn't want to have to answer. Subtly, on this short walk from his darkened home to hers, the climate between them had changed, tensed, lost its easy buoyancy. Nothing between them would ever be quite the same again. She remembered catching that one look of his which had warned her, and now his very silence was saying so. He had come to a threshold which he hoped she would cross with him as he wanted. And she couldn't, *couldn't*, though hating to hurt him, and dreading the aftermath of the reserves and embarrassments which must follow, spoiling their ease with each other for as long as they had to work together.

She noted with relief that both Dorice's car and Ysanne's were outside the bungalow. There was no sign of Arnot's. At the door Adam handed over the lamp and stood looking at her, still in silence.

"You haven't time to come in?" she asked.

"No. Sorry." He paused, then put a finger to the peak of the hood of her raincoat which she had drawn over her hair. "D'you know, this thing, and that –" pointing to the lamp – "make you look like a cross between Red Riding Hood and Florence Nightingale.

Trouble is, I don't know which I ... love best." He paused again. Then, "You know, don't you? That I've had it coming to me for some time?" he urged.

She fingered the lamp. "No. I —"

"But you knew tonight? Between there —" his head jerked towards his own bungalow — "and here?"

She owed him the truth. "I think so," she said. "And I was afraid."

"Afraid, love? Why?"

"Because of all it would change between us, and it mustn't."

"Nor need it. On the job — professionalism is my middle name. Off it — haven't we the right to be people? It's always happening to folks who have jobs in common. Why not to us?"

She hesitated. "It's not only because of the job," she said.

"Why, then?" He waited. "Or are you saying none of it has happened for you?"

"Not ... not in the same way as for you, I think."

"How do you know?" he urged. "I mean, how do you know it wouldn't, if I'd ever dared to show you? I never have. I thought you would say it was too soon, and you're not the sort of girl a guy tries it on with at the drop of a hat. It wouldn't have been fair. But since *I've* known, it's been tough — holding off, playing brother, timing the moment when — Why, I've never even kissed you good night. Until now — And this isn't just saying good night. It's asking; and telling; nothing brotherly about it at all; showing you — Yes?"

His arms about her were gentle, and though his kiss made a statement which said nothing to her heart, by contrast with Arnot Lord's violent assault upon her lips, there was comfort in it and a balm which her pride sorely needed. So, though guiltily, she relaxed within Adam's hold; not yet able to hurt him, she made no effort to reject his embrace.

Which was why, when the headlights of Arnot's car raked the enfolding darkness, showing them up, she sprang away from Adam as if they were lovers, startled by the intrusion upon their intimacy.

Arnot brought the car to a halt and got out. "Sorry," he said perfunctorily. "Don't let me interrupt anything."

Adam frowned, then grinned. "No offence taken. Just a spot of poor timing on both sides," he said easily.

Honor, despising her need to explain her errand, said, "I went to borrow this lamp from Adam; we hadn't so much as a candle." After which they stood, an awkward triangle, until, as had happened once before, it was Adam who was forced to give ground.

"Well, good night and bless," he said as he touched Honor's cheek, lightly claiming her. Arnot said nothing; merely waited for Honor to go ahead of him into the house.

Drawing conclusions – as he was entitled to. Drawing conclusions and, getting the wrong answer, not caring either way, Honor thought, foolishly longing to believe he had outstayed Adam deliberately ... laying his own claim, stating the primitive rivalry of one male for another, however little he valued the woman in dispute.

As it was, it was clear he wasn't bothering to comment. He thought he knew all that Adam's possessive little gesture had said. And knowing, did not care.

Adam was as good as his word. The next day, as he and Honor dealt with the patients in the clinic, no one would have guessed that his question to her was still unanswered, though she was only too aware that the answering – since it must come – was something she did not want to face.

Expecting that he might ask her to go out with him in the evening, she played for a little time, mentioning casually during the morning that, as it was the end of the month, she must return after siesta in order to bring the patients' cards and benefit records up to date.

Adam queried, "Must you – tonight?"

"I must, yes. I'm behind with them, and you know how Personnel flaps if they aren't on his desk on the stroke of eight a.m. on the first."

He nodded. "O.K. Duty before pleasure. It happens to the best of us," he agreed, making that his only hint that, as she had guessed, he had had other plans for them both for the evening. It was rather typical of his own dedication to the job that he didn't try to dissuade her. Or was it that he felt he could afford to wait to woo her? Wondering, conscious that she was being unfair to him, she wished she hadn't resorted to excuse. But his equable acceptance of it meant that she couldn't take it back now.

On her return that evening she had been working for some time when, to her surprise, Adam came in.

"Sorry to interrupt, but we've a call to make," he announced. "The wife of one of the mineworkers has had an accident. I can ring back from the site for an ambulance to bring her back to hospital, if it's necessary. But meanwhile, I'm taking you along. Ready now?"

"Of course." She collected and locked away the records she was working on and went out with him to his car. "What kind of an accident?" she asked.

"I'm not sure. I'd switched the phone through to my place, and Taju took a not very lucid message while I was out. A fall, I gather, so it could be anything from broken bones to a bruise or two. But one can't take chances," Adam replied.

Their destination, Koum, was an encampment of wooden huts, rather than a village. It centred round the mine-foreman's office, itself only a wooden shack, owing, Adam explained, to the fact that the miners lived a gypsy life, moving on from site to site of the nickel workings as the output demanded. As always, in the villages, children ran to surround and finger the car. As always, Adam had a tin of sweets ready for distribution, and as always he was given news of his patient in shouted *beech-la-mar*.

"She much bad, Mastar Doctor!"

"She fall heavy – so!"

"Ladder, him bad, rotten wood." And from a sceptic, "She not bad 't' all, the fat *popinée*. She only make like hurt, so her man fear she finish, make him sad . . ."

In this case the facts were that the woman had indeed fallen from halfway up a ladder, had cut her forehead, was badly shaken and bruised and had a hugely puffing wrist which Adam diagnosed as a probable sprain, rather than a break.

110

Helped by Honor and to a chatter of advice from the woman's assembled relatives, he splinted and bound her wrist, joked with her about the rainbow hues she could expect from her bruises, gave her a sedative and phoned from the foreman's office for her to be fetched for X-ray the following morning.

The little encampment stood with its back to the mountainside and as Honor and Adam came out of the hut into the dusk, one of the men standing by glanced up at the purplish haze which hung round the upper peaks.

"Mist no good, Mastar. Him come down soon," he warned Adam.

Adam got into the car. "In rain again?"

"Maybe rain. Maybe mist. But before night, f' sure. Bad then, 'long road. Telling you."

Adam said, "Thanks, but we haven't so very far to go. We'll beat it, I daresay."

They did – for just so far along a clear road as made the mist's swift descent a real shock. One minute it wasn't there, the next it was, swirling and wreathing, causing Adam to check, almost halting the car. He drove on more carefully, slowing down again as the mist thickened, putting on speed when it lifted patchily.

They met no other cars, nor expected to on that lonely road after the rains and at that hour of evening. But just as they ran out of comparative clarity into more mist, on Honor's near side there was the harsh scream of tyres answering to too-late braking, the long rasp of metal tearing at metal; another car bucketing and rocking from the impact with their own before with a judder it was made to right itself and tear on into the mist which folded down on it, losing it to sight.

Adam stopped, swore and glanced into the turning from which the rogue car must have come.

"The fool! The criminal fool!" he raged. "Taking a junction – *any* junction at that speed, and in this! Did you see the driver? Could you describe the car –?"

He broke off at the small whimper of shocked sound which was all Honor could manage. Then she heard herself falter, "L–Light-coloured. A m–man driving –" before the pain in the arm she was nursing became almost unbearable, making her cry *"Don't!"* to Adam reaching for her, and the dark of unconsciousness came down, blotting everything out.

She came to in a room she knew – the salon of La Voile. Her eyes focused slowly; on Adam, his fingers at her wrist, taking her pulse; on Arnot, looking down at her; on Mrs. Lord sitting beside her.

She smiled at them weakly. "Silly –" she said. "What happened?"

Adam said gently, "Silly is right. You'd carelessly left your elbow around for that road-hog to hit. Don't you remember?"

"Oh – yes." She thought back. "It was so hot, and I was resting my arm, with the elbow right out, on the edge of the door. You mean he caught it, and I – passed out?"

Adam nodded. "Out cold, almost as soon as I'd stopped cursing. But from shock as much as anything. The jolt they took, either your shoulder or your elbow might have been broken. But you're lucky, love.

Neither of them is, by my diagnosis. So – a night under sedation and an X-ray tomorrow to make sure, and you should be all right, except for a mass of bruising."

Honor said, "Oh –" and looked about her. "How did I get here?"

"How do you suppose? When I took my bearings, I realised we were within half a kilometre of Dorice's home, so here is where I brought you." Adam turned, echoing Arnot's question to him, "Where did it happen? Oh, back on the Koum road, where a side road from Koje comes in –"

"Koje Corner?"

"That's it. This maniac shot out, grazed us all along on Honor's side and was away. We didn't get his make or number, though his car should have at least as bad scars to show as mine has – *if* he made it much further without another crash." Adam turned back to Mrs. Lord. "Now may I get Honor to bed and see her comfortably settled before I leave?" he asked.

"Of course." Mrs. Lord rose. "But must you leave, Dr. Page? We can put you up, you know."

Adam nodded his thanks. "But I must get back. I'll be over again tomorrow to take her in for X-ray."

"Then come, dear –" But as Mrs. Lord was about to help Honor to her feet Ysanne came in, looked in startled surprise at Honor, then sank into the nearest chair, her forearms limp on its arms, the picture of exhaustion or shock.

Mrs. Lord paled and murmured, "*Mon dieu!* More trouble? Ysanne, *chérie*, what –? Honor has been in a car crash, but surely not you too?"

To that Ysanne's reply was to reach for Arnot's

hand as he hurried over to her. Holding it to her cheek as if for comfort, she said, "No. Not seriously, that is I – I'm just shocked, I suppose. It *was* my car. I mean, there was this other car. It just loomed up in my mirror, giving me no room and scraping all along the side of mine before it drove on –"

"Where was this?" Arnot's question cut in sharply. "On the Koum road, by any chance?"

She looked up at him blankly. "On the Koum road? Why?"

"Because it just could be the same car that crashed Dr. Page's at Koje Corner."

"At Koje Corner?" Between the first and second words of Ysanne's little echo, her glance caught Honor's across the room, her hesitancy of no more than a moment's duration before she went on, "Koum? Koje? Heavens, no. I was coming back from Port Maré by the diversion – in quite the other direction from either Koum or Koje. No, it was nothing really. It was simply that I was shocked and –" her eyes widened in appeal to Arnot – "and that I've been dreading your thinking that the damage to my car might have been my fault."

"Nonsense. You were able to drive it home? Yes? Then shall we go and inspect the damage?"

They went out together, while Honor, under protest, was gently propelled to bed in the room she had occupied on her week-end stay at La Voile. When she was settled in a borrowed nightgown and dressing-jacket from Dorice's wardrobe, Adam came with a sedative pill to be taken before she slept, and Mrs. Lord went to order the light supper he said she might have.

She heard his car drive away. Her arm was less painful now and already, before she had taken the pill, her senses were pleasantly drowsing. Her brain was trying to remember ... to question something. What was it? Something she hadn't understood at the time and now couldn't place accurately enough to wonder why it worried her.

Or could she? It suddenly dropped into place in her mental picture of the salon. Adam. Mrs. Lord. Arnot. Ysanne telling her story. Ysanne's hesitation before rejecting Arnot's suggestion that her accident had happened on the Koum road, somewhere near where the rogue car had crashed Adam's; her swift assurance to Arnot that she and her car had been somewhere quite other at the time.

Ysanne had needed to think quickly. Honor's intuition was convinced of it. Though why should there be guilt in her having been on the Koum road? Unless there hadn't in fact been two collisions, but only one ... one involving her car and Adam's; hers, the runaway into the mist, and her fear of admitting as much to Arnot, the cause of her lie?

Honor closed her eyes, summoning her memory of the moment of the crash. The other car – small enough for Ysanne's runabout, the same light colour, but driven by a man. A passenger beside him? Honor couldn't have said. But if he had had one, and *if* the passenger had been Ysanne, mightn't the driver have been the man Germain Trèves, her clandestine date of last night?

It all fitted. Rather too well? Honor hoped so, but, feeling sickened, she feared not. For if it were so, it meant they were all Ysanne's fools, and hating the role for herself, for Dorice, for Mrs. Lord, she knew she hated it most for Arnot, who trusted Ysanne to the hilt . . . loved her?

At the whisper of a knock on the door Honor glanced that way with a smile, expecting Mrs. Lord's return.

But it was Ysanne, a-tiptoe, who came in. "Tante Rachel sent me up with your handbag," she said. "But you hadn't closed it, and I didn't bother, and I'm afraid I dropped it on the stairs. I think I picked up what fell out − your lipstick, a comb − but if you'll check that anything else is missing, I'll go back and look for it."

"Oh, thank you." Honor sat up, took the proffered bag and riffled through it while Ysanne stood watching. "No, everything is here," she said, and again, "Thank you," before closing the bag and leaving it on the coverlet beside her.

There was a moment's silence. Then, as Ysanne turned away. "How are you feeling now? Anything you want?" she asked.

"Much better. A bit doped, but I feel I shall soon be asleep. How are you, yourself?"

"Oh, I'm all right. It was only the shock, and Arnot doesn't blame me at all. He wanted me to describe the other car, but I couldn't. Could you describe the one that hit you?" Ysanne queried.

"Not clearly. Except −" Deliberately Honor held the other girl's glance − "Except that it was small, white or cream, and was driven by a man."

Ysanne tapped the back of her fingers to her mouth,

as if to check a yawn. "Oh well, could be the same, I suppose, given he had time to do the distance between where he hit you and where he hit me. And if he was the same, and Arnot traces him, I pity him. For when Arnot saw what he had done to my car and might have done to me, he was mad enough to draw blood –"

When she had gone Honor lay very still for a moment before she reached again for her bag, opened it, felt for the corner of the pasteboard in an inner pocket and drew out the small square of card; a snapshot of Piers in bathing-trunks, his handsome head back, laughing into the sun.

The bag was a spare one which she didn't use often. When she had destroyed everything which could remind her of Piers, she had missed the contents of this pocket – a coloured shell from the beach where she had taken the snapshot, the snapshot itself.

The little shell would have said nothing to Ysanne. But if she had glimpsed the snapshot – what? *If* she had seen it, she could surely not have failed to recognise Piers as its subject? Therefore she couldn't have seen it, or she would have challenged Honor's possession of it; asked bewildered questions; shown all the jealous hurt which would be natural in the circumstances.

And so she had not seen it. The pocket had kept its secret. Or had it? And supposing Ysanne, for some devious purpose of her own, had chosen to allow her discovery to bide its time, what then?

CHAPTER VII

HONOR took that question with her into her drugged sleep, but when she woke in the morning the likelihood of Ysanne's having seen the snapshot without saying so seemed too remote for real worry. Much nearer home was the problem of how much – if anything – she ought to tell Dorice of her suspicion that Ysanne had broken faith with the promise Dorice had wrung from her, by going out again with Germain Trèves.

In the end Honor elected for silence. Having no proof, she was reluctant to accuse Ysanne, merely on her own sixth sense that the girl had lied to Arnot; lied to them all. True, Dorice had the right to expect Ysanne to honour their bargain. But Ysanne had an equal right to the benefit of the doubt which clearly was only in Honor's own mind, no one else having questioned the truth of her story at all. Honor resolved to hold her tongue.

Molla brought rolls and coffee to her in bed, and Mrs. Lord came to tell her when she might get up. When she went downstairs, her arm still in its padded sling, Arnot was at the telephone and signalled with an uplifted finger to halt her as she passed.

He replaced the receiver. "That was Page," he said. "He had made an appointment for your X-ray, but suggested he must cancel it, as he's been called out on a case and couldn't fetch you in time for you to keep it. But I took the liberty of offering to drive you to it myself, if that's O..K by you?"

It occurred to Honor that, since she had been at his side, he might have asked if she wanted to speak to Adam before he rang off. But as it evidently hadn't crossed his mind, she merely thanked him and asked him what time she had to be at the hospital in Port Maré.

He told her, and had his car at the door a quarter of an hour later. Mrs. Lord came to see them off, but to Honor's relief, there was no sign of Ysanne.

As they drove she wondered whether he was remembering, as she was, the upshot of their last tête-à-tête journey out from La Voile. Almost certainly not, she warned her hope. For whatever had been the motive of his first light kiss, he had intended the brutality of the second to dismiss her as a woman. He had said so, hadn't he? And meaning it, had written off the whole incident from his thoughts. Which explained his ease with her on their trek up-country with his mother; explained his cool acceptance of her since. No backlash of emotion. No undertones. Last night, coming upon her and Adam at almost the same spot of the very same threshold, he wouldn't even have been making comparisons between Adam's embrace and his own. By then, feeling nothing at all towards her, even contempt.

His voice cut across her thoughts. "I suppose, if I drew the obvious conclusions from my intrusion on you and Page last night, you'd think I was impertinent?"

Unseen by him, her fingers clenched into a fist. "No," she said.

119

"Then may I draw them? Though if I'm right, and Page is courting you seriously, don't you see some difficulties ahead?"

"Difficulties?" she echoed.

He glanced at her momentarily. "Well, surely, if you have marriage in mind? He is established in his job, a resident here, whereas you make no secret of meaning to shake the dust of Grand'terre from your feet as soon as your option is up."

"And can you wonder at that?" she queried, her tone dry.

"In the circumstances, no," he agreed. "But you see my point that without being frank with him, you could hardly expect Page to understand your reluctance to make your permanent home here with him?"

Honor drew a long breath. "Now you're not only drawing conclusions. You're jumping ahead of them, not to mention jumping ahead of the facts," she said.

"Which are?" he invited.

"One – that Adam Page isn't as much of a fixture here as you think; he sees Grand'terre as only one of several steppingstones on his way back to general practice in England. Two – that any question of my marrying him hasn't come up –"

"– Yet?" Arnot cut into her pause.

She compressed her lips, stared straight in front. "It hasn't come up," she repeated.

He nodded, laughed shortly. "I see. The snub direct. Perhaps I asked for it," he said, and allowed the silence to draw out.

She expected he would drop her at the hospital and said so. But he told her he would wait, and when she came out he drove her out to the U.N.H. plant and went into the bungalow with her.

"They will pass the results of your X-ray to Page, I suppose?" he asked.

"So they said, but he doesn't expect it to show a break." Honor paused and glanced at her watch. "Will you stay for a drink? Or for lunch? Dorice should be in soon for it."

"Just a drink. But you're handicapped. I'll pour my own, if I may. And for you?"

In essence, he was as far distant from her as if she were alone, thought Honor, as they sat side by side on the patio with their drinks. Handing her her glass, he hadn't an idea of what the casual brush of their fingers meant to her; nor the sound of his voice; nor the turn of his head her way. For her this was precious time stolen. For him, an idle interlude in his day.

He finished his drink, pushed his glass aside and stood up. "By the way, you're sure the car driver who hit you was a man?"

Surprised by the sudden question, Honor started. "Oh – why yes, quite sure," she said.

"You're convinced of that? The sexes look much alike these days. For instance, when Ysanne drives with her runabout open, she often bunches up her hair and wears a man's peaked apache cap on the side of her head."

Ysanne! Ysanne! Had he to quote Ysanne in comparison with every situation which arose? "Ysanne would have had hysterics." "Ysanne wears so-and-so." Ysanne, this. Ysanne, that ... Was her image so imprinted on his mind that he used it as a measure for

121

everything? Wondering so, Honor's flash of petty, impotent jealousy snapped back at him, "Well, this driver was a man. Hatless, young, I think, but a man. No question of that at all."

He looked surprised by her vehemence. "So you said, I know, and I wasn't doubting your word — only your sight, which could well have let you down at a moment like that. So it's definitely a man we're looking for. That narrows things down by fifty per cent, doesn't it?" he commented.

"You — mean to pursue it?" she asked faintly.

"Of course. Two near-crashes in the space of about half an hour — he might have killed any or all of the three of you!"

Honor shook her head. "I'd doubt that. I got the impression his was the smaller car, and in any full collision with Adam Page's, I think he'd have come off the worse. And anyway, isn't it Adam's headache, rather than yours, following him up?"

"In the case of his own car, yes. In the case of Ysanne's, it's very definitely mine — do you mind?" Arnot enquired smoothly, as Dorice came out on to the patio from the house, demanding the Hows and Whys of the whole affair. And while Arnot was there, listening, Honor had no choice but to keep to her decision to voice no suspicion of Ysanne's broken promise to Dorice. Later she might confide in Dorice. But not yet, while there was still no proof that the girl had been out again with Germain Trèves.

The chance of her accident gave Honor a brief grace from the need to give Adam his answer. For when her few days' sick leave from the clinic was over, she knew he would ask her out again, and this time she mustn't refuse him, however difficult the outcome for them both. She found herself wondering how she had managed to snub Arnot so tautly on the subject of Adam, when she knew then, as surely as she did now, that Adam's courtship was honest and serious, asking of her all that he brought to it himself. What a lot it would solve, if she could echo his tentative "Yes –?" with a heart-warmed "Yes" of her own, instead of the "No" she must give him, and still have to work with him as before!

On the morning she returned to duty, he was already at his desk, reading his mail. He had disposed of the usual crop of medical pamphlets and advertisements and was deep in what appeared to be a personal letter. He looked up from it at her, his smile at once a welcome and a caress.

"So? Back to the treadmill and all systems go?" he quipped.

She smiled back. "And not before time, judging by the pile of stuff dumped on my table. Not to mention the returns I never finished for Personnel the other night."

"Yes, well – polish them off first, and you can take your time over the rest." Adam paused. "And off the professional beam while we're alone, would you feel equal to a quiet dinner with me tonight?"

She looked away. "I'd like that," she said.

"Right. I'll call for you. I'm not quite sure when I can make it. But wait for me."

They dined in a quiet restaurant that was new to

Honor. It was on the outskirts of the city, and when they came out Adam swung on to a road which climbed towards the lower slopes of the mountain chain. "Coffee, liqueurs and all the solitude we need at a little *auberge* I know," he announced, sounding as if he were making of the evening a happy promise to himself.

On the way Honor told him about Arnot's return to the subject of the rogue car, and of his determination to track down its driver for Ysanne's sake.

Adam commented, "Then with the little there is to go on, he'll need more luck than I've had so far. Just your glimpse of the driver and Ysanne's sighting of the car before it grazed hers. And that's odd too –" He paused, frowning.

"What is?" Honor queried.

"The damage to her car. I could be wrong, but as I remember, she told us the other car showed in her mirror, scraped the side of hers and drove on." Adam paused again. "*In her mirror,* mark you. That means he was overtaking; she couldn't have seen him in her mirror otherwise. *But* her car was still standing out when I left La Voile that night, and all the scraped paintwork was on the wrong side. Not a blemish to be seen on the other. Odd, you'll agree?"

Honor worked it out. "The damage was on the passenger's side?"

"Where it couldn't be, if the driver were overtaking."

"Unless he were driving so wildly that he overtook on the near side."

Adam shook his head. "If he had been as crazy as

124

that, wouldn't she have said so? No, if I heard her aright, it was a normal overtaking, except for the fellow's criminal speed. Which, as it makes a nonsense of that damage, I couldn't have heard her aright. Q.E.D., as the saying goes. Though you heard her too. What do *you* think she said?"

Honor hesitated. "I'm – not sure." But as Adam agreed, "No, of course you were a bit dopey at the time," she knew she was only too sure. That the damage to the near side of Ysanne's car had been caused by its having been turned into the path of this one – Adam's – near side to near side at the point of impact, and therefore – one accident, not two, and that one at the reckless hands of Germain Trèves. This was proof. This was certainty. Ysanne *had* made dupes of them all.

The courtyard of Adam's little inn, set about with rustic tables, lighted by oil-lamps, was empty of any customers but themselves. Adam went inside to order for them both, and when he came back he reached for Honor's hand, playing idly with her fingers while they waited to be served. But when, later, he began, "Something I have to tell you –" it wasn't quite what she expected to hear.

He said, "That letter I was reading when you came into the clinic this morning – remember? Well, it was from an uncle of mine, one half of a two-man general practice in a country district of the Cotswolds. His partner has just had to pack it in, because of heart trouble, and Uncle Trevelyan has offered the vacant partnership to me. If I decide to take it up, he can give me a fair time in which to join him, but not so much before I give him my yes or no. But if I agree, you see what that does to the plans I remember outlining to you once, don't you?"

Honor nodded. "You mean you would be leaving Grand'terre much sooner than you intended?"

"As soon as I could get my release from U.N.H., and my initial contract with them is up in a couple of months. But more than that – I shouldn't be footloosing it about the world as I'd meant to, before settling down. And that –"

"And that you would regret?" she put in.

He reached for her hand again. "Don't put words into my mouth, d'you mind?" he scolded gently. "What I was going to say, madam, was – 'And that is where you come in, my love'. Meaning – if I do decide to team up with Uncle T., can I hope you'll marry me and come back to England with me – prepared to settle down too?"

She looked at him, her eyes shadowed. "Oh, Adam, I –"

"The other night, before this England bit came up, you knew I was going to ask you then? You let me kiss you as if you knew."

Guiltily she remembered how gratefully she had yielded to the comfort of his arms. "I thought I knew," she admitted. "If not about marriage, I knew you – wanted me."

"Well, I said so, didn't I? *Was* telling you so with everything I have, when we were rudely interrupted. This is just the sequel that has had to wait. And though you said then it hadn't happened for you, now I've shown you what *I* could make of loving you . . . marrying you, doesn't it happen for you a little? Can't it?"

She shook her head, ashamed. "Not in any way that would be fair to you."

He was silent, biting his lip. "I see. You don't love me as I love and need you. But then people never do love quite equally, and couldn't you let me judge as to 'fairness'?"

"You think you can now, Adam. You wouldn't always."

"I'd risk it."

"You might for yourself. Not for me. I couldn't and mustn't marry you, not loving you as I should."

"*Should!*" His fist thumped the table. "Have there to be rules about it . . . degrees? And I thought –"

She touched his clenched hand, felt it relax. "I know. When you kissed me, I let you. I was touched that you should want to. I was grateful. It had been so long since –"

"Since you'd been kissed?" he prompted.

"For love – like that, yes."

"Then it's true – what you told Dorice and she passed on to me – you were engaged once and the fellow jilted you?"

"He dropped me because he was engaged to someone else and he went back to her."

"This happened before you came here, and because of that affair you can't love me? But you mustn't hang on to the rags of the thing like that! It's morbid; I've got to believe you've more courage than that!" Adam protested.

She nodded. "And you can. I didn't hang on. But it's not a kind of equation – that, not loving him, therefore I can love you enough to marry you. You do see?" she appealed.

His mouth wry, he agreed, "If you say so. Though if there's been no one else for you since –" He broke off at her almost imperceptible movement. "Or has there? *Is* there?" he pressed, and when she did not reply, "Some man who hasn't kissed you for love, as I did, but who is 'for you', all the same? For you, on your side; maybe not on his? And that's why you're turning me down?"

Disarmed by his perception, she said weakly, "Now you're trying to make another equation. Please leave it, Adam. I like you so much. I've never worked with anyone I've respected and relied on as I do you, and we're such friends. But none of that is enough for marriage, as you must know well."

He took her up. "Liking. Respect. Friendship – all good solid things that'll last a heck of a long time, wouldn't you say?"

"But not without the love that we *both* ought to feel, thrill to . . ." As Honor spoke she was hearing an echo – "Someone, long ago, knew that marriage without love is just so much bare rock –" Mrs. Lord's whimsy, remembered from the one magical day when Arnot had been companionable, relaxed, even impersonally gentle, as never until then, nor since. She came back to the present to hear Adam asking,

"In other words, you know you could thrill to this other 'for you' chap? And there is one, isn't there? But out of reach – why?"

"Just – out of reach."

Adam said heavily, "And that's all you're telling.

128

You know, I didn't think, in these days, that two people could get to our stage of – let's call it accord – with one of them, me, believing so blindly that he wouldn't be turned down?"

"I'm sorry, Adam!"

On a note of bitterness he said to that, "Don't be. You can't help it, and 'Sorry' is such an empty word." Then he added more evenly, "Anyway, I'm left in no doubt, am I, as to what I shall be saying to my uncle T.'s offer?"

"You'll be going back to England – because of me?"

"I'll be going back to England – full stop. No names, no packdrill." Whatever it cost him, he grinned in his accustomed puckish way and ran his hand lightly up her arm from wrist to shoulder. "Thanks for the hope at least," he said. "It was wonderful while it lasted," as he brushed her lips with his own. Forgiving her, she knew.

She expected he would take her back and want to leave her at once. But he ordered again for them both and as full night came down he challenged her to a game of naming the stars and constellations they each knew. It was late when they left at last, Bruce driving by a route which took them through the paraphernalia of warehouses, Customs sheds and chandlers' stores which made up the city's dock area. By day it was char-acterised by a raucous, frenzied busyness. At night, ex-cept for the sailors' bars in the canyon-narrow streets which led down to it, it was a dead place, its still air heavy with a mingling of the smell of harbour water, the sickly odour of the copra loadings and the musky tang of the sandalwood stored in open sheds, adjacent to the quays. Its lighting was from the riding-lamps on the craft in the harbour basin and from neons high on the tall warehouses, beyond the range of which the shadows were deep.

It was from one such shadow that a figure suddenly reeled, hands outspread as if to ward off the dazzle of Adam's headlamps, before it rocked back again, hit a wall and slumped to the ground.

Adam uttered, "Tchah! A drunk!" braked and got out. Ordering Honor, "Stay where you are," he went across to the man, bent over him and came back at a trot.

He reached for his medical bag. "He's not drunk, but he must have been in a fight. He's bleeding from a long gash from his elbow to his wrist, and though he isn't saying how he got it, he has told me where he lives. Have to get him there when I've fixed his arm. I know the place. It's only a stone's throw, but it's a tenement in an alley that's too narrow for the car. Sorry about all this, but it's lucky for him we happened by. You'll be all right until I get back?"

"Yes, of course."

"Good girl!"

After he had gone and presently had hauled the man to his feet and trundled him away, the area was quiet again, except for the intermittent burst of accordion or piano music when one of the neighbouring bar-doors opened and shut.

Honor was hoping that it wasn't from any such haunt that Dorice had had to collect Ysanne on the night of the storm when a second man's figure loomed up alongside the car, but this time a sober, casually strolling one, a mere belated passer-by.

But he didn't pass by. He glanced at the stationary open car, hesitated, halted, then approached it on Honor's side to peer curiously at her face.

She experienced a pulse of fear. She should have gone with Adam! "Yes?" she queried shakily. "What do you want?" – only to be disconcerted by the stranger's short, throaty laugh.

In the slow sing-song drawl of Grand'terre he said, "Don't you know me? We haven't exactly met, but you've seen me before, I think. And I know *you*. You are the medicine-man's little friend, aren't you? Go driving with him on every excuse you can, h'm? Remember me now, mademoiselle?"

Honor did. Though she would have said her sighting of the driver of Ysanne's car had been an impression, rather than a view, her instinct confirmed what he was telling her – that he was Germain Trèves and he expected her to recognise him.

She said gravely, "Yes, I remember you. Some nights ago you were driving Mademoiselle Faudron's runabout. At a junction with the Koum road called Koje Corner, you grazed Dr. Page's car and drove on. He didn't get a glimpse of you, but I did. As, it seems, you know I did, though I don't understand why, when you didn't come forward at the time, you should be admitting it to me now?"

"M'm," he drawled. "Was in two minds about it, I'll give you that. But then I thought – Always as well to know your enemies and just how much harm they can do you if they're so inclined. A bit curious too as to why you haven't been disposed to tell on me. Because you haven't yet, have you? And I ask myself, Why not?"

"Simply because I had no proof the driver was you. At that time I didn't know you, even by sight," Honor said coldly.

"And now I've handed you the proof, what are you going to do about it? Tell the world? Get pretty little Ysanne into trouble for daring to snatch a bit of fun on the side from that V.I.P. of hers who is willing to take her over at second-hand from Piers Sabre rather than not get her at all? Because that's all I'm bothered about – that she shouldn't be blamed for a bit of harmless joy-riding with me."

"Harmless?" Honor took him up. "You couldn't care then that you caused an accident which could have been serious, and didn't stop?"

He snapped a finger and thumb. "Pff! A bagatelle, that. I'd get a fine for careless driving – no more. But I had to know how much you knew and could tell, if you chose. So I decided to show my cards and find out. For the babe's sake, you see –" He paused. A shaft of light caused his black eyes to glitter as he went on, "Not, you ought to know, that the little one wouldn't be a match for you herself, if you did turn telltale on her. Knows something about you, she says, that *you* wouldn't care to be made public, any more than she'd like Big Chief Lord to know about her and me. How about that, mademoiselle?"

Honor felt her blood chill. With her voice barely in control she said, "Do you know, that sounds as if you were threatening me? *What* that's unsavoury does Ysanne Faudron think she knows about me?"

132

Trèves lifted a shoulder in a shrug. "She wasn't telling."

"But she knows too that I had recognized her car?"

"Guessed as much, yes."

"Then I wonder either of you risked my not saying anything to Dr. Page."

He shrugged again. "Worth it, according to her. No point in admitting she was out with me, supposing you hadn't recognized the car. And if you had, and did tell, at least she could pay you out." He straightened and stood back. "Law of the jungle – live and let live, see?" he added with an insolent grin as he turned away.

Honor watched him until the shadows swallowed him up. *The snapshot of Piers in her bag!* Ysanne must have seen it, recognised him. For that was the only damaging thing she could possibly know and thought she could use. But hadn't yet. Why not?

Adam came back, explaining that he had thought it best to see his patient to bed before leaving him. Mechanically Honor asked, "Will he be all right?" and for the rest of the journey hoped that the talk she exchanged with Adam was making sense.

She was glad that he was willing to leave her at the door of the bungalow; also that Dorice wasn't at home. (How was Dorice going to judge her when Ysanne told her story?) Making haste to get to the privacy of her own room before she had to face Dorice, Honor almost missed the message for her on the telephone-pad.

Dorice had written,

"Arnot rang, asking for you. Told him you were out for a jolly with Adam. Nothing that mattered, he said. Just that you had left a headscarf in his car when he

brought you in for your X-ray that time. See you –
D."

Puzzled, Honor thought back, convinced she hadn't
left anything in Arnot's car that day. As she tore the
sheet from the pad and crumpled it, the telephone
rang. She lifted the receiver, gave the number and said
"Yes. Speaking –" to Arnot's voice questioning,
"Honor?"

He said crisply, "I got Dorice when I rang earlier,
making a necessary excuse for asking for you. Now I
need to see you. But not here at La Voile and not at
your bungalow. Alone. When are you free? For instance, if I arranged to pick you up at the U.N.H. main
gate tomorrow at noon, could you be there?"

She hesitated. "Y– yes, I think so."

"Good. We'll lunch somewhere. I'll expect you."

He rang off and she replaced the receiver. This was
her doom, her notice of expulsion, not to be staved off.
Ysanne had told Arnot what she had learned, and now
must be placated, reassured, disarmed, comforted. By
Arnot.

She'll have demanded my head on a charger and
been given it, thought Honor bitterly. Grand'terre,
Dorice, Mrs. Lord . . . Arnot – presently they would be
the mere memories she must make them, after she had
gone away, hounded by the cruel chance which had put
Piers Sabre in her way when a happier fate might well
have sent her to this lovely island, uncluttered by the
past, free to be herself, to make her own appeal –

Arnot's own words, those, she remembered. Spoken
tellingly but without kindness in his effort to persuade
her to hold her tongue for Ysanne's sake. Dimension.

Shape. Attractions. Might she have had them for him too if she hadn't met and trusted Piers first?

Bleakly she realised that she would never know.

CHAPTER VIII

THE next morning, before they closed the clinic for the siesta hours, Adam said, "By the way, may I ask you to keep it under your hat that I'm cutting adrift from my contract here?"

"Of course I will," Honor promised him. "You'd rather even Dorice didn't know as yet?"

"Better not, until I've handed my official notice to the powers-that-be." As he ushered her ahead of him and locked the clinic door, she ventured, "You've fully decided to go, then? You – you wouldn't consider staying, supposing *I* left at my own six months' option to go?"

"Go?" he echoed. "You? Why on earth should you think of leaving so soon? You've made friends here; you enjoy every minute of your job, and off-duty, you're a natural for a fun-place like Grand'terre, which should have everything going for you. *Go* – when, compared with me, you've hardly arrived? You really have to be joking on that!"

She managed a wry smile at his illogicality. "Last night you wanted me to leave when you did," she reminded him.

"Ah, but *with* me. As my wife. Or, if you'd wanted to, I'd have gone along with staying myself. No, *I'm* going with good reason – because, without hope of you, I could keep up the professional bit for only just so long. Nothing, I warn you, permanently brotherly or platonic about me —" He broke off. "And that's below the belt, too. I promised no packdrill, didn't I? Forget it."

Honor looked at him gratefully, almost tempted to tell him that for reasons he couldn't guess, she *would* be going too; that already her time on Grand'terre was measured by the terms which Arnot would dictate when she kept her rendezvous with him within the next few minutes. But she had to let the impulse go. She could tell Adam nothing without telling him everything, and that was forbidden to her. For, purposeless as was her pledge to Arnot, now that Ysanne must have learned the truth, the letter of it still held; a spoken promise which she hadn't yet the right to break.

She and Adam reached the point where the paths to their quarters divided. As always here, he lifted a careless hand to her. "See you —" he said. And as always she quipped in their jaunty password — "Not if I see you first!" But this noon, she knew, he stood looking after her, watching her walk out of his future.

He was volatile, good company, made friends easily, and he would not remember her with regret for too long. But at that moment, for guilt's sake towards him, she could not trust herself to look back.

Arnot's car was already waiting when she went out to the main gate. Considering the urgency and secrecy with which he had summoned her, she had to admire his polite restraint in greeting her. They might have been casual acquaintances, meeting for a luncheon date, instead of partners in a deal which had blown wide open too soon. From this side of its exploded weakness she told herself she ought never to have allowed him to persuade her to it. But the first step taken, she had followed him blindly; jealous of his motives, but going all the way with them ... even being able to love him for his deep care for other people which made use of her connivance without apparently questioning his right to ask it of her.

She was surprised that he should risk lunching alone with her. But he had taken care of this too by telling her he was driving her out into the country to an inn where he was not known.

He said, "I couldn't go into details over the phone. But I had to get in touch with you urgently. Ysanne knows who you are, and you had to be warned, because from here we have to watch our step. You know –" he paused, frowning – "I could have expected you to destroy every bit of evidence which might link you to Piers. But it appears you didn't. Do you realise you left around a snapshot of him for Ysanne to find and draw her own conclusions? Well, do you?" he urged irritably when Honor did not reply at once.

"I–"

"So you did know she had seen it, though she didn't let you know she had?"

"I didn't know for certain at the time." (She couldn't tell him that, through Germain Trèves, she did now.) "Ysanne handled a bag of mine one day, and I'd overlooked the snap of Piers in an inner pocket. I knew there was the risk she might have seen it. But when she said nothing –"

"For pity's sake!" The ball of Arnot's palm thumped the steering-wheel. "When you realised there was the faintest risk, why didn't you tell me ... warn me?"

Honor said dully, "If she hadn't seen it, there was no harm done. If she had, I'd have expected her to accuse me to my face; certainly that before now she would tell someone – your mother, Dorice, you –" Realising that his sympathies would be all for Ysanne, she added, "Was she very upset when she did tell you?"

"Upset? She was beside herself. What do you think?"

"I – I'm sorry."

"So am I," he confirmed crisply. "Our pact deserved more than sheer carelessness, and I could better have picked up the pieces if I'd been warned beforehand. As it is, I had to act fast to ensure that Ysanne's suspicions of you don't go any further."

Honor turned to stare at his profile. "But she must have told Mrs. Lord too!"

"No. And she won't attempt it while she has to admit that, as she caught only a glimpse of the snapshot and can't produce it, she has no proof that it was of Piers. Accused, you could deny it ever existed, or claim it was of another man friend of yours, not of Piers at all. Your word against hers, and she isn't risking that."

"Why not? As an argument, it's very thin."

"Of course, and it wouldn't have persuaded her without the backing of a stronger line. Namely, that as you must have supposed that the whole of Piers' family and his friends would have heard your name, was it likely, I asked her, that you would have dared to show up on Grand'terre. Or, having come and met any of us, have brazened it out."

Honor countered, "But *you* believed I had done just that – followed Piers here deliberately."

Arnot threw her a swift glance. "That was before I knew you."

"Not 'before'," she murmured.

The jerk of his head was impatient. "Don't split hairs. Say I've revised my view of you since. Anyway, though I don't pretend Ysanne may not be watchful of you and you may be embarrassed in her company, I'm convinced she'll hold her fire while she's not sure of her ground. I take it you don't mean to outstay your option to leave U.N.H.?"

"Of course not. I can go after giving them a month's notice." As Honor's thoughts flew to Adam, she was half tempted to defend herself against Arnot's indifference by adding, "If I decide to go back to England instead of to Australia, I might leave when Adam Page goes." But she had given her word to Adam that she would say nothing of his plans, so that even that rag of pride was denied her.

Instead she puzzled aloud, "Since Ysanne knows the truth now, why persuade her she doesn't know it?"

Arnot glanced at her again. "Can't you guess?" he parried.

(If only she could believe he was genuinely concerned to protect *her*!) "No," she told him disspiritedly.

He said, "Oh, come. For all the existing reasons. Dorice has accepted you; values your friendship. My mother has grown fond of you – too fond to be hurt by still having to see you around. I'm thinking for

140

them, as I am for Ysanne. If you hadn't been so careless, she would have been spared unnecessary pain too."

Stung, Honor retorted, "You don't spare me much reproach, do you? And how do you know I mightn't want to make my peace with Ysanne – tell her before I go that she has no need to feel jealous or embittered towards me over Piers: that he had jilted me as he jilted her; that –"

Arnot cut in drily, "But you won't tell her, because I forbid you to. At the price of my mother's peace of mind you aren't sloughing off any guilt you may feel over Piers by 'confessing' to Ysanne. You gave me your word, and you are keeping it until none of it matters any more. Understood?"

"Once I've gone, then it won't matter any more," she said, making a statement of it.

"*When* you've gone, let's say it will matter less to everyone concerned. That's life. It moves on." With the first spark of warmth of interest he had shown her that morning he added, "For you too? You'll have some regrets at leaving the island?"

She nodded. "A – great many."

"Some personal ones, I'd hope. Even for us – Piers' family?"

Tempted, she wondered what he would say if she replied, "For all of you" with emphasis he couldn't mistake. But all she must allow herself was the candour of her eyes as she looked at him and said with deliberate evasion, "Particularly for anyone I've wronged. I've told you I'd have liked to ask Ysanne to forgive me over Piers. But that, you say, you won't have."

"That," he echoed, "I won't have. What's more, I

suspect you're hedging. If you do leave Grand'terre alone, you'll leave other personal issues rather open-ended, won't you?"

"Meaning?" Her tone was discouraging.

"Page, of course. Have you had to acknowledge that I was right — that you owe him a frankness about yourself which you can't let him have? Can't, that is, before you go."

"*Needn't*, before I go. Nor, possibly, ever," she corrected. "You really should not read so much into so little evidence of an affair between me and Adam Page, you know. You may have heard gossip. You've seen him kiss me. So what of it? There are good night kisses *and* good night kisses. As you should know," she added with a flash of malicious meaning which she thought could not escape him.

It didn't. From the swift jerk of his head she could almost see his memory at work. He said evenly, "You couldn't resist that, could you? But all right — point taken. I *should* know, and the next time I kiss a woman with any more purpose than I'd kiss the back of her hand, I promise you I'll make very sure that we both know what it's all about. Enough said?"

It was one of "those" questions. Snubbed, she knew he did not expect her to reply.

At the inn where they were to lunch she went ahead of him on to a terrace, feeling that food might choke her, but sensing he would refuse to take her straight back instead. Their host was a morose Jack Sprat of a Frenchman; his wife garrulous and as plump as he was lean. She had no other customers, served their meal herself and lingered to gossip between courses.

142

Taking them for tourists – in which Arnot did not correct her – she listed for them all the island sights they ought to see. Before they left Grand'terre they must see or experience this, that, the other and, assured by Arnot that he intended they should miss nothing, she played her trump card.

A *bounia* now? They had not attended nor been invited to a *bounia* feast? An occasion which many passing tourists hadn't the opportunity to enjoy. But as it happened, a *bounia* was being planned in this very district shortly, and if they cared to avail themselves, she, their hostess, would see they were invited. A privilege, yes. Not every European was welcome –

Arnot thanked her, asked the date of the coming *bounia* and regretted they would not be able to attend. Madame commiserated with them on that, bade them au revoir, and in the car Arnot enlightened Honor as to the nature of a *bounia* feast.

"It's a Kanaka alfresco get-together, and our friend was right – it can be a privileged affair. It's age-old; it would originally have been held to celebrate an occasion – the birth of an heir to a chief, or peace talks with an enemy. But nowadays it's more in the nature of a Harvest Home or merely because someone thinks it a good idea to hold a *bounia* and the thing catches on."

"What does *bounia* mean?" Honor asked.

"It's the pièce-de-résistance of the feast – a parcel of almost anything that's available and edible, wrapped up and cooked for hours in layer upon layer of banana leaves. Meat, veg. – the mixture has to be sampled to be believed. You may have a chance to see –"

"*I'll* see?"

"Before you leave, we might persuade the Kanaka workers to lay one on for you on the estate. Say, to celebrate our excellent copra season. Something. We shall all have to attend."

"All? But *I* can't be there. I can't come to La Voile again – now!" Honor protested.

"Because you can't meet Ysanne? Nonsense. It won't be easy for you, but how can you afford suddenly *not* to come again whenever Dorice wants to bring you or my mother asks you?"

Wondering whether he could have any idea of the ordeal it would afford her, she said, "Anyway, you shouldn't ask it of Ysanne."

"While she has no proof against you, nothing is being asked of her that isn't the lesser evil to the petty lies and evasions you would be put to, and which neither my mother nor Dorice could be expected to believe. In any case, if we hold a *bounia*, it will be a crowded, public affair; on that occasion at least, you and Ysanne can easily keep your distance."

He dropped her where he had picked her up at the gateway to the plant and she went back to the clinic, convinced that only in work could she quieten the turmoil of her thoughts. Before she left that evening she composed, typed and made ready her letter of resignation from her post.

As it happened, she was to be spared the delivery of the letter.

When she was summoned unexpectedly to see the Personnel Officer, she was offered the New South Wales posting if she cared to take it after a re-shuffling of staff which would be completed a month hence. U.N.H. was prepared to give her that month in which to decide whether or not she wished to make the move.

Though she did not need the time she accepted it. Destroying her letter of resignation, she was glad to be rid of the sense of guilt she had felt at throwing over her job after only six months in it. But Dorice, being told, took a very poor view of her change of plans. Why on earth, Dorice wanted to know, had Honor come to Grand'terre at all, if she hadn't meant to stay for the full term of her contract? What was wrong with the island, for pity's sake? With her job? Wasn't she happy here? If not, why not? People had made her welcome. She was "in" everything, wasn't she? And – not least of Dorice's grievance – whoever took Honor's place would be loaded on to her, Dorice, as a housemate. Did Honor even *care* about that?

On the latter score Honor could be reassuring, as she understood her post was to be filled by someone who was married to a local U.N.H. executive. But though she pointed out that she had had no choice about being sent to Grand'terre, and that U.N.H. itself had forestalled her resignation, Dorice was not placated to any degree. It was the first rift in their friendship and without any open differences, they drifted a little apart. Now Dorice did not always press Honor to go with her to La Voile when she went back herself, and though Honor missed the gracious, friendly atmosphere there, her regrets for it had to be mixed. For with Ysanne at La Voile, knowing what she knew, it was now a dangerous place.

Now she spent more of her leisure with other people

– with Adam on the easy level of friendship which he had now accepted, and with his cronies of the moment. They saw more now of the Frenchman, Jean Salinger, and of his varied girl-friends, with regard to whom Jean claimed wickedly that he kept a card-index of names, characteristics, jobs and preferences, so that he shouldn't mistake Carole for Alice, or Yvette for Eunice or Nathalie.

"Eunice?" Honor mused one day to Adam. "Wasn't she the young New Zealander who had dinner with us one night way back?"

Adam nodded with a grin. "The very same – come back into Jean's young life. They don't often... Seems her people are leisured and rich and Mama has been induced to bring Eunice back for a second holiday this year. What's more, Jean wants you and me to play gooseberry again – this time for a two-night motel camping over on the East Coast. This next weekend. What do you say?"

"You mean Mama is willing?" marvelled Honor.

"I gather so, with us two greybeards as chaperons. Say you will. It could be fun," Adam urged.

It was. The camp site was beside a river; wide lawns shaded by palms and the tall columnar pines which gave the region its name of Kunie. The two-bedded cabins were minute, grass-roofed beehive shapes; meals were taken al fresco or in the long cool bar of the main building. There were canoes and clay pigeon shoots and fishing by day, and dancing and river trips by cable-drawn ferries by night. Most of the other campers were young, and on both nights it was well into the small hours before Honor and Eunice got to bed in their dolls'-house of a cabin.

Eunice, happy and relaxed, proved quite an endearing companion. Naïve and negative in a crowd, she opened up like a flower with the one or two people she liked to be with. Discussing them, Adam and Honor wondered how, in the social melée in which Jean moved, he should ever have noticed her; much less have singled her out; less still have wanted to see her twice. Adam declared it could only have been the challenged of wresting her from Mama, but Honor maintained it was the attraction of opposites – that Jean, mercurial and worldly, felt the irresistible pull of Eunice's calm orbit, a theory which was borne out by Eunice's shy confidence – "Jean says I'm different," she told the darkness and Honor when they talked for a long time after going to bed.

And then Eunice, all unwittingly, opened a door which had been closed ... She said casually, "Dorice Sabre is the name of your housemate, isn't it? I wondered, has she a brother or a cousin in New Zealand, do you know? Because, a while ago, at a party back home in Napier there was a boy named Sabre, Piers Sabre. I remember the unusual name –"

Honor shot up, propped on her elbow. "*Sabre?* You're sure?" she demanded, and at Eunice's nod, "Yes, if he were in his early twenties, he could be Dorice's twin. Did you talk to him or get to know him?"

But Eunice hadn't. They had been introduced and the French-sounding name had struck her, but they hadn't met again. "What does he do over there?" she asked.

"I don't know. His family doesn't. Nor even that he is in New Zealand, I think." Honor realised that in relating Piers' disappearance after his break with Ysanne, she must not appear to know too much of things that had happened before she herself came to Grand'terre, but inwardly she was shaken, wondering what this news would do to Arnot's view of their pact when she passed it on. Meanwhile she allowed Eunice to suppose that she would tell it to Adam and of course to Dorice, though in her own mind she was resolved that Arnot must hear it first.

Her immediate problem was how to reach him privately with it, but Dorice helped in this with a now rare invitation to La Voile.

"I've news for them and I may need some moral support," she announced in asking Honor for one evening after the camping trip which sent back Eunice, happily confident that Jean would want to see her again.

"News? Am I in on it?" Honor asked.

"You are now. I'm briefing you beforehand. I'm giving in my notice here and taking off for Europe about at the time you leave yourself."

"You *are*?" breathed Honor. "I know you told me you meant to, and I'm so glad for you. But will your people mind?"

"They could. You know what families are. But that's why you're coming along – all enthusiasm and as a shining example of a girl's doing her own thing. After all, you cut free of your family when you wanted to stay out here, and I daresay you aren't any less fond of them, as *I* shan't be of mine, just because

I want to travel, which means snipping the apron strings. You'll back me up?"

"Of course. As far I can." Honor paused. "But Piers, Dorice? Does this mean you despair of his coming back? Supposing he did, and you weren't there?"

As usual at her twin's name, Dorice's face clouded, but her tone was hard as she retorted, "If he does, that'll be just too bad. I'm not going for ever – a year, at most two, and the way things are, I could wait till doomsday and he'd never come back." She changed the subject. "By the way, I'm not too keen on Ysanne's being at the family pow-pow. It's nothing to do with her, and if I know anything, she'd be pitying me for not getting married instead. *Married!* So as she'll be out tomorrow night, we'll go over. Suit you?"

As it always was, Mrs. Lord's welcome of Honor was warm. It was Honor's conscience which detected a faint reserve in it since Dorice must have reported her decision to leave. Though the older woman was too well bred to show it, Honor sensed her disappointment that a girl she liked had proved a fly-by-night after all.

On the whole, Dorice's plans were better received than she had expected. There was surprise and demur from Mrs. Lord, but Arnot's reaction was mainly practical – "What are you going to use for money?"

"Savings," Dorice retorted promptly. "And when they run out, there's always work. I'm a qualified secretary *and* a good one. They're needed anywhere, even on board ship. And I shouldn't be surprised if there weren't a golden handshake from my chief. He claims to approve Enterprise with a capital E."

"Even at the loss of an obviously self-satisfied secretary?" Arnot queried drily.

"Remains to be seen," Dorice had to admit. "But the middle-aged shouldn't pontificate if they don't expect the young to take them up." She rose impulsively and went to kneel by Mrs. Lord's chair. "Don't worry, Tante Rachel," she urged. "Grand'terre will always be 'home' to me. It's sort of in my blood, as it's in yours. I'll be back!"

After that there discussions of ways and means, clothes, passport, inoculations – all the exciting paraphernalia of a journey. It was a family conclave from which Honor was somewhat shut out. And neither Arnot nor his mother, she noticed, put her own question to Dorice – "Supposing Piers should come back?" In private, surely one of them would? But tonight he was not mentioned.

At last Dorice, well pleased, said, "May we have a party to wish me bon voyage?"

"Of course, dear. In fact, something was already in my mind," smiled her aunt, whose forgivable quirk was to appear always to have been the first to think of any welcome idea. "What would you like? Dinner here? A dance at the Club? A swimming party?"

Dorice considered. "Not just a dinner – a lot too square. Swimming – m'm. I'd rather it were something for everyone on the estate. Couldn't we –? *I* know! We'll hold a –"

"A *bounia*?" Arnot said through the smoke of his cigar.

"How did you guess? Could we?"

"Probably," he agreed, "if I put the word around

that the young ma'am is off to seek her fortune. It would have the advantage of saving us the organisation too. We'll merely foot the bill."

He and Dorice debated dates, while to Honor Mrs. Lord approved a *bounia* as being of the size of party to enable one to meet one's friends, at the same time avoiding one's pet enemies. Then Dorice, promising to call back for Honor, drove over to tell her friends, the Rozel brother and sister, her news; Mrs. Lord left the salon too, so that, for the short time she might be alone with Arnot, Honor had to use it fast.

She said abruptly, "I've something to tell you," and watched the alert jerk of his head. "Yes?"

"I think you can rely it's true. I've heard that Piers is – or was pretty recently – in New Zealand. In Napier."

"Heard?" Arnot echoed. "How?"

"At Kunie, last week-end."

"Yes, Dorice said you were on a foursome party which included Page. Well?"

Honor told him, concluding, "After all, a man of that age and description named Piers Sabre couldn't *not* be Piers –"

"And –?"

Honor gestured emptily. "That's all I know. It's all this girl could tell me. But you'll follow it up – try to get in touch with him, won't you?"

There was a silence. Then Arnot said, "No."

"*No?* But –"

"My reasons? Because Piers is no minor. I've no control over his movements. He knows where Grand'-terre is, and if he comes back or wants news of it or

151

any of us, it's going to have to be by the same will as he left it – his own."

Honor protested, "For Dorice's sake, for your mother's, for Ysanne's, you wouldn't lift a finger to trace him, even if you failed?"

"Given the right resources, I probably shouldn't fail. But do you suppose I haven't considered turning stones in search of him before now – always deciding against? Because, caring as little about any of them as he once did about you, what good would it do them – *any* of them – to get the dusty answer that he has no intention of coming back?"

Nervously unable to remain where she was, Honor rose and went over to the window, where she stood, fingering the edge of the undrawn velvet drapes. Although she knew he had followed her at a stroll to stand close behind her, she spoke only to the darkening garden as she said,

"How can you know he would refuse, unless you hold out the first hand to him?"

"At the moment I see no need to risk it. If he wants news or needs to give it, I repeat, he knows where we are. And you – as obviously you haven't yet – won't say anything of this to Dorice. Do you understand?"

Understand? Suddenly, blindingly, Honor thought she did. *He didn't want to trace Piers, lest Ysanne should want to take him back.* He needed his own field clear to Ysanne –

She said in a low voice, "You're cruel, and quite ruthless, aren't you?"

"Cruel!" he echoed sharply. "Does that mean *you* want to see Piers again?"

"I?" She looked up at him from over her shoulder. "*No!*"

"Ruthless, then. All right, I accept that, as long as I think my purpose is good."

"And use anyone in sight who'll serve your purpose!"

"Not just 'anyone', assuming that in our case you mean yourself. Anyway, one doesn't 'use' allies; one co-opts them." He paused. He was so close now that she could sense his breath fanning her neck, as he went on, "But I never had to ask the willing help of a woman before, which is probably my bad mistake with you, though you were the only ally to hand, and I couldn't help myself. But one should use different methods with women — more of the glove and less of the fist. I see that now, and I daresay you know what I mean?"

As his fingers went lightly to her shoulder and increased their pressure, she did. She moved quickly and his hand slid away. "I think I do," she said. "If I'd come to pattern or been anyone else, you'd have tried making love to me, and then I might have been — more pliable."

"Might have been. But never were, and aren't still. You and I, Honor Troy, set off on the wrong foot and we've been on it ever since. And now it's too late to —"

They both started almost guiltily as, at the flick of the switch, the full light of the centre chandelier came on as Mrs. Lord returned. She swept across to draw the cord of the curtains. The garden and the darkness were closed away; Arnot and Honor went back to their chairs; Mrs. Lord took up her tapestry-frame. They became three people sharing a social evening.

153

CHAPTER IX

THE day of the *bounia* was fixed; the enthusiasm of the Kanaka workers was fanned and from time to time Dorice enlightened Honor on what to expect.

"You could call it – in our case – a kind of outdoor office party on a huge scale. It'll begin around noon and go on until all hours," she said. "Don't wear anything that matters, for it can get a bit wild; anyway, it's only fair to leave all the colour and the finery to the Kanakas and *their* guests – it's their day. There'll be singing and dancing and mime, all a bit uninhibited, and eats and drink galore. I advise a crash diet beforehand, for you'll be appalled at the amount of food you'll be expected to put away."

"Where are you holding it?"

"Ours? In a coconut grove that runs down to the sea. Gives a chance to take off for a swim if you feel so disposed, or if the company gets a bit overwhelming. Our party probably won't stay on after dusk!"

The morning of the *bounia*, a Saturday, had a clarity of atmosphere which enhanced every colour and sharpened every outline. After a season of many days which had dawned in a haze of heat, it was not oppressively hot that morning. "A scrubbed clean" day, Dorice described it as she and Honor drove over to La Voile.

The site of the gathering was within walking distance of the gardens, and when the girls arrived they found the La Voile party had gone ahead of them, as had all the house and garden-staff as well. Even if they hadn't known the way they would have needed only the wafted smoke of the cooking fires and the ecstatic shouts and crowing laughter of the assembled guests to guide them.

Then in the great clearing there was colour – a blue glitter of sea between the boles of the coconut palms, the yellow of bordering sands and, outmatching Nature, the dazzling kaleidoscope which comprised the party warpaint of the crowds. Blues, pinks, greens, lilacs, all rioted in the shirts and headdresses of the men and the sarongs and shifts of the women and girl-children. There was embroidery and lace and ribbons and feathers and veiling – finery donned with a prodigality which was breathtaking. Clearly a *bounia* was an Occasion with a capital letter.

There was some dancing and a little singing – a spontaneous crooning which started up and then died away. People moved about, greeting and embracing their friends extravagantly, and everywhere children darted between and around the bare, graceful, satin-brown legs of their mothers and aunts and grown-up sisters. The earnest business of the day would be the cooking and serving and eating of the ceremonial meal, but even so early there was presented a selection of the dances which would become even more boisterous and realistic as the hours wore on and the available drink had been eagerly "taken".

Dorice went to join other friends, leaving Honor with Arnot and Mrs. Lord to watch a troupe of men and boys miming the shipwreck of a canoe.

155

They acted even the rising of the storm; mimed the failing efforts of the rowers to keep the craft afloat; at the very peak of suspense they allowed the wind to drop by the accompanying beat of the drums and tambourines being softened, and finally landed safely on a shore they had sighted from afar, but had never hoped to attain.

After that there were fishermen's dances and mock battles, with whirling slings and brandished spears for weapons, and love-dances in which the women took part, advancing and retreating with stylized gestures which spoke their own language of enticement without a word uttered.

It was late afternoon before the colossal meal was cooked and ready to serve. The seating arrangements were woven mats on the ground, and Honor sat between Arnot and Mrs. Lord as the preliminary courses of chicken and sucking-pig and fried crayfish preceded that of the traditional *bounia*.

The wrapping banana leaves of each portion were peeled away by the girl server, who hovered to offer condiments and to see that the warm, fragrant parcels were approved. The mixture today was of sweet potatoes, onion, herbs and chicken blended with coconut milk. Arnot sampled his bundle first and in dialect said something to the girl which made her blush and laugh. She replied in the same tongue, and when she had gone, Arnot translated, "I told her I hope the *bounia*-keeper – otherwise the cook – would serve the same recipe at her wedding, and she came back with a promise that she would see it was served at mine."

"Then I hope," remarked his mother, delicately

licking a finger, "that she will also make finger-bowls available, for a well-gravied *bounia* is the messiest dish in the world."

The richness of the earlier courses was offset by the serving of fresh fruit as dessert, after which the resulting débris was gathered up and the torpor of siesta overtook everyone but the children. Mrs. Lord, preparing for a sleep by lying back, but claiming that without shade for her eyes she couldn't close them, had searched in her bag for her sun-spectacles without finding them.

"You can't have brought them with you," Honor suggested.

Mrs. Lord nodded. "No, dear, and I believe they are in my tapestry bag which I left beside my chair in the sun room. Never mind. I'll find some deep shade instead."

But Honor was already on her feet. "I'll go back for them," she offered. "After that meal, I need the exercise!"

Back at the house all was silent. Honor went straight to the sun room, and was kneeling on the floor to search the bag's depths, when footsteps and a murmur of two voices sounded outside.

She knelt up and looked out, her kneeling figure hidden from view by the wooden lower half of the walls. The family always left their cars standing out, and immediately outside was Ysanne's runabout; at its side were Ysanne and Germain Trèves, who was coarsely handsome in tight denim trousers and widely open shirt. Ysanne was also in trousers with a daring halter-top. She carried a shoulder bag which, after a mo-

ment's hesitation, she shrugged off and threw into the
back seat of the little car. The sun-room door and the
wide hinged windows were closed, but a small open
louvre allowed Honor to hear the man's confident
chuckle as he glanced from the bag to Ysanne.

"Cap over the windmill? You decided to come prepared?" he taunted her lightly.

Honor watched Ysanne frown. Sounding nervy
and irritable, she snapped, "You know I always carry
a bag that size. Anyway, I —"

She almost turned away from the car, but he was
swift to clamp his fingers round her wrist. "You aren't
letting them get away with it, are you?" he urged.
"You're coming? You aren't backing down at this
stage, for goodness' sake?"

"Who's backing down? How dare you?" she
wrenched free of his hold, hesitated for another moment, then stepped into the passenger seat of the car.

Tréves looked surprised. "Letting me drive, h'm?"

"You may as well," she told him ungraciously.

"As you say. We'll make better speed that way, and
the old girl is expecting us —" But before taking the
driving-seat he went to lift the bonnet, which gave
Honor time to come to a decision and to move.

How dared they? had been her first bewildered
thought. How *dared* they, in view of Dorice's blunt
warning to Ysanne and the girl's own fear lest Mrs.
Lord or Arnot should learn of the affair? Where were
they going? And what was the ugly significance of the
man's quip as to the size of Ysanne's bag? Did he see
it as her — *luggage*? *And if so* —?

Honor stepped outside. "Where are you going?

What about your promise to Dorice?" She spoke to Ysanne, but it was Trèves who stepped to her side. Falsely bland, he said, "And what business is it of yours where we are going, *chérie*?"

Honor snapped, "I'm making it mine. Ysanne is breaking a promise by seeing you. I know she has already done it at least once, but if you leave together now, other people are going to know too. I mean that."

His stare was insolent. "Oh, get lost," he spat out. But Ysanne interposed, "She does mean it. She hates me. She'll go straight to Arnot and we'll be followed."

"When no one knows where we've gone? *She* can't stop us."

"She'll still tell Arnot, and if we're going, we can't let her."

"We've time on our side. She has got to reach him, and today she can't do that by telephone."

"We still can't *let* her," Ysanne insisted on a rising note.

"Then what?" he retorted irritably. "A kidnap? Take her with us –?"

Honor stepped back. "You dare try!" But he moved nearer. "We can, you know. Two against one. Get into that car!" He was thrusting her towards it now, and though she had no intention of being forced into it, on a sudden idea she ceased to resist. For he was right. There was no help at hand, and only by letting them take her as far as they would could she get any idea of their destination. At least she would learn the direction they took. She stepped willingly into the back seat; Trèves took the driver's, and steered expertly between the crowd of cars parked by the family's many guests for the *bounia*.

Evidently Port Maré was not their objective. Trèves took an up-country road, driving fast. Ignoring Honor, Ysanne said, "You must be mad, letting her spy on us. How far, before you drop her off?"

"Far enough for our purpose. Somewhere nice and remote, where she might have quite a job to thumb her way back. Anyway, far enough for us to be well on our way, h'm, honey?"

But Ysanne frowned. "You can't drop her off just anywhere. You should never have brought her. Now you'll have to take her right into—"

She broke off as his hand shot out to clap over her mouth. "She can make what she can of where I mean to drop her, but she's not coming *that* far. That'd give the whole idea away," he said sharply.

They were discussing Honor as if she were a parcel to be dumped and labelled "Collect", but she decided to keep a stony, remote silence, concentrating on landmarks on a road which was quite unknown to her. It was one of the countless byroads which climbed at gentle angles towards the foothills of the Central Chain, crossing many little rivulets nearer and nearer to their sources. She decided Trèves had only just stopped Ysanne from mentioning some township or large village where at least there would be a shop or post office with a telephone. But for many kilometres of the way there was no sign of anything of the sort – just the narrow road running snakelike between lush greenery for more than an hour's driving when the rain came down. The bright day evidently had been scrubbed too clean; its abnormal clarity had presaged rain to come, and now the rain was here – great coin-sized drops at first, and then the beginnings of the relentless downpour of the sub-tropics.

Trèves touched a lever, bringing the hood over the car and a few turns of the road further on, as Honor was debating the significance of his words about "the old girl", he drew up. Over his shoulder he addressed her, "Out, m'selle. This is as far as you go."

Honor remained in her seat. "I'm not getting out here," she said, and Ysanne protested, "Germain, you *can't*. Not in this rain! Now take her on to where she can –"

"She's getting out here." There was an ugly set to his jaw as he spoke. Pointing across a clearing to a ramshackle, obviously deserted beehive hut, "She can shelter – there, and hitch herself a lift as soon as someone comes by. This is the end of her line."

"Then it's the end of my line too. If you put her out, I get out too," declared Ysanne, and then spoiled this show of compassion by adding, "It's too late now. Arnot will have to know we brought her and left her, and what do you think that's going to do to me?"

Trèves shrugged. "Over to you. Your problem."

"Well, this is yours. You brought her. Now – do we go on, or do we both get out here?"

For a minute he allowed the hostile silence to brood. Then he drove on until he drew up at an isolated flat-roofed small house at the roadside. "Well, like it or nor, this *is* the end of the line," he said.

Ysanne stared at the house. "*This* is where you live with your aunt? But you said it was in Baresol!"

"Our address is Baresol. Ask the mailman. Well –

are you coming in or not?"

Ysanne scanned the outline of the house. "You aren't on the telephone," she accused him.

"Never gave you to suppose we were," he retorted.

"Then how is *she* to get back? It must be quite twenty-five kilometres –!"

"Would have been several kilometres less if you'd let me put her off where I wanted. It was your idea to bring her all the way, and now she knows the lot, we don't want her getting back *too* quickly, do we? That would spoil the fun."

Ysanne snapped, "*You've* spoiled the fun. You should never have brought her." She stared ahead, biting her lip. "Anyway, it's no good now. If your aunt is expecting us, I'll just speak to her, make an excuse for not staying, and then I shall have to drive Honor back myself." Again she scanned the blank face of the house, adding suspiciously, "Your aunt does know we were coming? She is at home?"

"Not just at the moment, no –" Trèves drawled.

"Not? Then where is she?"

"Staying with her sister in Port Maré for the weekend."

"Then she didn't invite me to stay the night? She didn't even know you were bringing me?"

"Not unless she has second sight. *I* didn't tell her. I did the inviting. You came of your own free will."

At that Ysanne became a fury, a primitive creature impotently hitting back. She turned on him. "You – you! You tricked me! You cheated! You said your aunt wanted to meet me, and I believed you, that she would be here to chaperone me. And I only came so that *they*

162

should worry about me, wonder where I was. For that I'd even have stayed two nights – or more. I didn't want you, you *gredin*! I never did. You've just been useful to me, d'you hear? *Useful*, that's all, and now you've botched the whole thing. And so –?" But as she made to take the car keys from him, he swung them teasingly at her, then dropped them into his pocket. "And so – what?" he taunted her.

She stared at him. "You can't! It's my car. Switch on again and give me those keys and then get out," she ordered.

He got out. "Useful as a chauffeur, h'm? Is that all? Are you quite sure? All right. I'll just be a chauffeur in future – *but* in my own time. I'm not stealing your car – you asked me to drive it and you here, and if you look in at the car-pound on Pont l'Eveque in Port Maré on Monday morning, say, it'll be there. And not my fault the thing went sour on us. If anyone's – hers!"

As the insolent jerk of his head indicated Honor, Ysanne turned to her too, tears of sheer rage in her black eyes as she claimed, "Not his fault! Not his *fault*, when he tricked me into coming and being alone with him overnight! I suppose he would have done the same thing then – seen to it that I couldn't get away!" Turning to him again, she spat another French vulgarity at him – "*Canaille!*"

But Honor, sickened by this slanging-match, had had enough. With a man of his type they couldn't win, and her instinct was to get both herself and Ysanne away from him at all costs. She alighted decisively from the car. It was raining less heavily now. "Come along," she ordered Ysanne. "You've said all you're going to say, and for the moment there's nothing you can do. So we're going," and she handed Ysanne's shoulder-bag to her.

"Going? *Walking,* you mean?" queried Ysanne incredulously, as if it were an exercise in which she never indulged.

"Walking back," Honor confirmed sternly. She set out, and after a vicious glance back at Trèves, standing beside the car, Ysanne trailed tortoiselike alongside.

They trudged in withdrawn silence for some time. Then Ysanne began to grumble.

In their flimsy sandals, her feet hurt. (So did Honor's.) She was soaked to her skin. (So was Honor.) Why hadn't they gone on into the hamlet of Baresol, wherever it was? (Because, Honor pointed out, they didn't know where Baresol was, whereas she had noted the way this road took.) She would almost certainly get pleurisy or pneumonia or something, and *then* they would be sorry, Ysanne claimed to hope – and lapsed again into sulky silence when Honor said drily, "And as I gather that was the object of the original exercise, then you'll be satisfied, I daresay?"

But as they ploughed on towards the nightfall which might come down on them before they were picked up, she realised the girl's frailer strength was flagging. They had long since passed the deserted hut where Trèves had wanted to discard her, but Honor remembered there was another ahead by, possibly, a half-kilometre, and promised Ysanne that they would rest there.

Between it and them, however, was one of the many rivulets which, when they reached it, Ysanne suggested they should ford, saving themselves two sides of a tri-angle of road by doing so. It wasn't deep and its bed offered boulders which could serve as steppingstones. But the boulders were weathered-smooth and slippery. Honor, going ahead of Ysanne, had difficulty in keeping her balance and Ysanne lost hers entirely when, within a handhold of the further bank, her foot slid down the rounded slope of a boulder, and she dropped into the shallow water, her foot bent under her.

She knelt up, whimpering hysterically, "It's my ankle. I've broken it, I know." And as Honor went back to help her to her feet – "I can't, I can't!" though with Honor's arm supporting her she presently managed to half-step, half-hop to the safety of the bank.

Certainly the ankle was puffing, but she had to be urged and propelled the now shortened distance to the empty hut, where her shoulder-bag was able to produce a headscarf which Honor used on the ankle as a triangular bandage. They sat on the rotting benches abandoned by the hut's earlier occupants and prepared for what Honor realised must not now be merely a rest but a vigil until some traffic approached from either direction on the lonely road. Ysanne couldn't go any further on foot.

For all their common plight, they achieved no friendly rapport. Honor was preoccupied with listening for any sound of wheels or an engine on the road, and for the most part Ysanne kept a glum silence which seemed to blame Honor by implication, as well as the "them" – Arnot, Mrs. Lord, Dorice, Honor supposed – against whom she had laid her shabby little plot originally.

165

Honor had wondered whether this be the time and place for Ysanne to accuse her about Piers. But evidently Arnot had impressed her with the folly of that without proof, for she said nothing, even though Honor felt she could only be biding her time. For as today's abortive meanness showed, Honor judged Ysanne didn't forgive easily, if at all.

The rain came and went and the brooding storm clouds darkened the evening prematurely. It was night indeed inside the hut when the long-awaited sound came – a car approaching on the road, its lights raking from beyond an adjacent bend. Honor dashed out, both arms signalling widely. The speeding car crew up; its driver craned forward; a voice – Arnot's – said, "Honor? What are you doing here? I'm looking for Ysanne –"

(She hadn't returned to the *bounia* with Mrs. Lord's sunglasses; by now she must have been missed. But it was *Ysanne* he was seeking in headlong haste – always Ysanne!) In spite of herself the mean thought stabbed through Honor's mind, but now Arnot was out of the car, almost shaking her by the upper arm. "*What are you doing here?*"

"Ysanne is here too. In there. She has sprained her ankle," Honor told him.

"You are together? And why here?"

She could have asked him the same question. Of all the roads and byways in the island, that he should choose this one in search of a missing Ysanne! But then she remembered that Dorice knew of the affair with Germain Trèves; which made Dorice the link in the sorry tale; Arnot employed Germain, so would know where he lived, and the deductions which had brought Arnot hot-foot must have been made from there.

But now he was at the hut door where Ysanne, hobbling and drooping towards him, was ready to be swept into the cradling hold of his arms. Without questioning her, he carried her to the car and though she whimpered a protest that she would be all right sitting beside him he supported her in the back seat and showed Honor into the front. Evidently he knew enough to be able to postpone explanations from Ysanne, but of Honor he asked, "How did you come to be mixed up in all this? When you went back to the house you weren't missed for hours, because Maman found she had her glasses with her all the time, and sent someone – young Molla, I think – to tell you so. When you didn't come back, she concluded you had joined some other party, and it wasn't until we all left the *bounia* much later that Dorice noticed Ysanne's car had gone and it emerged that neither of you had been seen since siesta. Trèves was at the *bounia* of course, as he had the right to be, but I gather that you knew, as Dorice admitted she did too, that Ysanne has been seeing him clandestinely. Is that so?"

Honor said, "Yes, I knew."

"But you were prepared to cover up for her, even though Dorice at least knew the type he is? Why?"

Embarrassed that they should be discussing Ysanne as if she were not there, Honor said, "Because she appealed to us both not to tell you or Mrs. Lord."

"Tcha! Schoolgirl loyalties!" His exclamation was irritable. "And this afternoon –? What about that?"

Honor told him. In the course of the story Ysanne sat forward to protest, "I didn't *mean* anything by it, Arnot! I wasn't eloping with him. He tricked me. He told me his aunt —" to which Arnot replied snubbingly, "All right. Leave it. I'll settle for Honor's version now," leaving a chill in the air which in Honor's experience he rarely allowed to touch Ysanne; reflecting his sense of outrage that she could betray his faith in her so.

As they neared La Voile there was an unwonted glow in the sky and the rhythmic thud of many feet and drums showed that the *bounia*, for all its damp evening, meant to continue far into a night of revelry under the stars of washed-clean skies. At the house itself Mrs. Lord and Dorice were waiting; Dorice ready to accuse and reproach, and Mrs. Lord deeply concerned to see Ysanne straight to bed.

"Post-mortems tomorrow, not tonight," she ordered firmly. "Whatever she has done, the poor child is quite worn out," — and had her way, conveniently ignoring Dorice's mutter of "Nuts to 'worn out'. What about Honor? And the rest of us — worried to the shank of our wrists over the little so-and-so?"

Mrs. Lord was away a long time and when she rejoined the other three she wore a strange air of deflation, even of shock. Unseeingly she sank into the chair Arnot offered her and rested her head on her hands, shading her eyes; then lifted them, bright with starting tears.

She said quaveringly, "She hates us, Arnot! She says so. She wants to go away — to leave Grand'terre. If it weren't for her ankle, she declares she would go

168

tomorrow. But anyway, as soon as – Leaving us, hating us. Arnot, how can she, after all we –?"

"Hates us, does she? By what right? Because of – Piers?" It was Dorice, her voice hard, who wanted to know.

Mrs. Lord shook her head. "Not because of Piers. I think she hated us almost as much before that – even hated *him*. Because when he came back from Australia, wanting her, asking her to forgive him for a – silly infatuation he had already put behind him, she wouldn't listen. She says she laughed at him for supposing she would take him back. She – she repeated the dreadful words she used to him. She called him a 'secondhand man' and threw her ring at him and broke with him then and there. *She* broke with *him*, and we – *we never knew!*"

CHAPTER X

THERE was a stunned silence. Then, as if Arnot sensed that Dorice's anger was at flashpoint, he gave her something to do by indicating the drinks tray. "Pour a brandy," he said, and himself took it to his mother, holding the glass for her until she was willing to sip from it.

Presently she steadied, drawing herself up. "I forbade you to question Ysanne, and I didn't mean to either," she said. "But she *would* talk. Not sadly, nor ashamedly – more as if she had been hoarding it all against us for a very long time and was enjoying the effect of hurting us, as she calculated it would. Even Honor –" Mrs. Lord paused and looked over to where Honor sat, hands folded in her lap, nails dug into palms, waiting . . . "She hadn't even any mercy for you, my dear, after all you did for her today! She had to hint there was something about you which you wouldn't want us to know, and though I'm glad to say I ignored that, she would persist, saying, 'Ask Arnot, if you don't believe me. He may tell you. He just may –' "

Arnot glanced quickly at Honor, then back at his mother. "Empty hints against Honor only? But about the rest of us she was more direct?"

"A great deal more. Dorice has always been jealous of her, because she had come first with Piers. Piers had no backbone –"

"Backbone and decency enough to shield *her* from what we'd all think of her, if we'd known she had turned him down!" Dorice exploded.

"– And I," went on Mrs. Lord, "have always treated her as I would a lapdog or a kitten. I – I wouldn't let her grow up. Nor would you, Arnot, she said. You've always been as careful of her as a man should be of the girl he'd like to marry, and *she* realised you, not Piers, were the man for her, even while Piers was in Australia. She has done all she could to show you so since, but you've still only been cotton-wool-soft with her, when you should have been passionate. And that was the reason for this man Trèves – she didn't care for him any more than she did for Piers. He was aimed at you, even though she daren't tell you about him. She was flaunting him to herself, showing off that she was adult enough for you to care for her in the way she wanted. As she was convinced you did until –"

"Until?" Arnot prompted into the pause.

"Well –" His mother's eyes met his candidly. "Perhaps this is where I'm to blame, if not for the rest, at least for today's escapade with that man. You see, that she wanted you was no news to me. I'm old enough to recognize infatuation when I see it. Not necessarily love, you understand. People can mask that and often do – sometimes disastrously, until it's too late. But desire that has to display and preen and assert itself, as Ysanne's has done for your benefit, is something yet again. And as I didn't want her hurt any more than I had to hurt her by telling her, yesterday – *was* it only yesterday? Yes – So I told her."

171

"You told her what?"

"Simply that I knew you better than she did. That you could be kind and you could pity, but that you would never marry for less than love. That you had done what you could to console her for Piers's rejection of her, but that, child as she is, she must know that in marriage pity is not enough."

Arnot said hardly, "You took a great deal upon yourself, didn't you, Maman?"

"No more than, at the time, I saw as my duty to the child. *Any* mother, knowing her son's character, would have done the same, and Ysanne had to know some time – hadn't she?" Mrs. Lord appealed.

It was a direct challenge to his agreement which Arnot ignored. Instead he asked, "And what was Ysanne's reaction to your third-party diplomacy, one wonders? Wasn't she hurt?"

"Hurt? But of course. What do you think?"

"She needn't have believed you –"

"Ah, but she had to. She ought, deep down, to have known I was right – that for a marriage to survive, there must be love on both sides, and while we talked then, at least I thought she was only hurt – which would pass. Not – not that she was already planning the sort of petty vengeance on us all that she has shown today. And she isn't even sorry, at that. She – she's like a cornered animal – spitting and fighting back. She would do as much tomorrow, and worse if she could, she says."

"And you can believe that," put in Dorice. "She's all kitten-tricks, without a grown-up impulse in her life. And we've let her play us along – pandered to her, been

172

sorry for her, smoothed her down –! "

"That will do! " Arnot cut across the tirade. He took the brandy-glass from his mother and set it aside. As he turned back – "And the result tonight? You say she wants to leave the island now? Where for? "

"France, she says. Paris. You know she has an aunt there with whom her stepfather had quarrelled, so that there's never been any connection since he brought Ysanne out here. But she thinks the aunt would welcome her now, though of course there's the question of the money for her fare to Europe."

"She really wants to leave Grand'terre for good? "

"She says so. Among other things, the women are all prudes and the men are boors. She has always been misunderstood here, been unloved. Whereas in Paris –"

"Then the mere matter of the lack of the air fare to Europe shan't stand in her way," Arnot cut in harshly. "As soon as she can walk on her ankle, she's free to leave. Tell her that, will you? Or no –" he stopped Mrs. Lord with a hand on her arm. "I'll tell her myself in the morning. We've things to say to each other, Ysanne and I."

"I'm going to miss her, all the same." Mrs. Lord rose slowly and turned away. But Dorice was quickly at her side, an arm about her.

Dorice said urgently, "You mean you're going to miss your *idea* of her, Tante Rachel! We know now she never was what we all thought her – the darling doll we all had to shield. We've picked her up, and dusted her down, and wiped her tears and, yes – I've even lied for her before now. I know why you wanted

173

to love Ysanne – because you wanted a daughter, and I didn't quite fill the bill. But now, d'you know what? – I'll give up the thought of Europe and stay here instead! Not much good, me, at mere daughterhood, I'm afraid. But I will stay and I will try, I swear I will, if it will make up to you for Ysanne in the least little way?"

But her aunt's response was only to pat her gently on the cheek and to smile. "No, you'll go, dear," she said. "Nobody can play daughter – or sweetheart or wife or any role at all – that is a false one in their own eyes. No, you, *chérie*, should see yourself just as a branch of our family tree with the right to grow not only up, but *out* and away in search of whatever kind of light you need. You don't have to break away in consequence –" Mrs. Lord's glance drew Honor into the talk for the first time. "Isn't that so, child?" she asked her. "When the sap was rising in you, you allowed your home to leave you? I know it is usually the other way about, but either way, a going, a journeying, a leaving, a parting – none of them have to mean an open break, have you found?"

The appeal took Honor unawares, but she was grateful for it. She has been surprised that the three of them should have cared for her to share a family scene that was so intimate and poignant for them, when they could have asked her to leave. Why hadn't they? she wondered as she answered her hostess sincerely, "No, indeed they haven't. My people and I are as close as ever we were. I shall go back –"

"And I shall *come* back," declared Dorice roundly. But for them all, Honor felt, there had to remain the thought of the two rebel branches which had broken, not merely grown, so rudely away.

Yet Arnot almost certainly had it in his power – he had said so – to trace Piers. She had thought, it now seemed wrongly, that he hadn't done so for jealousy of Ysanne.

So would he now? And if not, why not? Who could be hurt now by Piers' return if he were willing to come? Surely no one?

Neither Dorice nor Honor saw Ysanne again before she left the island. Dorice had avowed that she wouldn't be responsible for her reaction if they had to meet, and Ysanne was probably as little anxious to see Honor as Honor was to see her. They had done with each other, she and Ysanne, and when neither Dorice nor Mrs. Lord pursued the hints which Ysanne hadn't been able to resist levelling against her, she was grateful for whatever code of honour towards a guest kept them from doing so.

Meanwhile, Grand'terre time was running out for Adam Page and Dorice as well as for herself.

Dorice's evenings were a mess of maps, brochures and sailing-schedules; half-finished sewing and experimental packing to see how much she could cram into the two duffle-bags and a shoulder knapsack which were the total luggage she was willing to take. Adam was busy, reporting on his stewardship of the clinic and training his successor. Of the three, only Honor had few preparations to make for her going – an airline ticket to Sydney, a suitcase packed overnight – and when the day came, Grand'terre and all it had meant to her would be behind her for good.

Then, a few days before she was due to sail, Dorice was summoned to dine at home one evening.

"Tante Rachel rang me at the office," she told Honor. "I was pretty busy and she was rather vague. Some guest they have – or was it guests in the plural – not sure – who wants to meet me. I said O.K., though I didn't catch who they were, or from where. Just flown in from somewhere, I think. Tante Rachel didn't mention bringing you, though I daresay they'll find you a crust to gnaw if you care to come. Do you?"

But Honor had promised to return to the clinic to help Adam with some filing of patients' records. "And afterwards," she told Dorice, "I'm going to wash my hair."

Dorice grinned. " 'The best laid plans . . .' " she quoted. "Don't tell me our Adam won't have the decency to take you out afterwards."

Which indeed Adam suggested as they packed up after a couple of hours' intensive work, and with nothing before her but her appointment with a shampoo, Honor accepted. She was comfortable with Adam now. He had settled for her friendship and no more.

As they took their seats in the small Indonesian restaurant he had chosen, he had news for her. "Believe it or not," he challenged, "friend Jean may have made his last date with the assorted dollies of the island. He has been invited to take his vacation with the Eunice-child's people in Napier, and he has accepted!"

Honor laughed. "No? Meeting her folks? Has that ever happened to him before?"

"In my acquaintance of him, not if he could help

176

it," Adam grinned back. "Looks to me as if he and that dewy infant are going steady now, though. Funny, isn't it," he mused, "how the unlikeliest people sometimes strike sparks that light up, when the really good friends may not make it?"

"There has to be friendship too," Honor said quickly.

"'Too' – yes. But that doesn't mean it's enough. If it were, you and I –" Adam broke off there, adding, "All right. Don't worry, love. I'm not spoiling what could be one of our last dates."

They talked about Ysanne's departure, Adam not above reminding Honor that he had summed her up while everyone else had been willing to let her walk all over them, as he put it. "From all accounts, she even had Arnot Lord as her slave," he claimed.

(*As her slave perhaps, but not, it seemed, as her lover.*) Ever since the night of the *bounia* when Arnot, tight-lipped, had appeared even more disillusioned than his mother, Honor had cherished a little irrational warmth in her heart. She had been wrong. He didn't love Ysanne. He had merely – as they all had – allowed her to use him for pity of her. Not that his indifference to Ysanne Faudron added up to his feeling anything at all for a girl named Honor Troy. . . . So that the warmth must fade. But while it lasted, it was comforting.

Adam was questioning, "I think both you and Dorice believed Arnot was in love with Ysanne, didn't you? Weren't you surprised when, as you've said, he was only too ready to let her go?"

Honor agreed, "I was, yes. I thought –"

Adam held her glance. "Gratified too? Glad? A bit – *happy?*"

She blushed and looked away, unable to answer him, and for a long minute he respected her silence. Then he said slowly – "So? *He* was the chap 'for you', though you not for him? The 'out of reach' we talked about and you wouldn't tell me who? Oh, my dear –"

Honor managed to summon a shaky laugh. "I know. Idiotic, isn't it? I should have seen it coming; never have let it catch up on me –"

"But it's why you're going back to Australia, when you could have stayed here for two years at least?"

"Yes."

"And clearing Ysanne from his decks hasn't done anything for you?"

"No. Why should it?"

Adam nodded agreement. "No reason, of course. The man either loves you or he doesn't." He paused. Then, "This is breaking a promise, I know, but you still won't let me try to make up to you for it all? Come to England with me as my wife?"

She looked at him with swimming eyes. "It wouldn't work, Adam. Not fair –" Embarrassedly, she had to sit back and fumble in her bag for her handkerchief as their waiter came to the table, bending to speak to Adam.

"The telephone, sir. You are wanted."

"A-a – h!" Adam muttered an expletive and rose. "I forgot to tell you I'd agreed to be on call tonight for the Martin-Gurnay practice in the city. If it's a patient of theirs I have to go to, I'm afraid we must cut short and leave." He rose, adding, "No, finish your coffee,

178

while I go and find out what's wanted."

When he came back Honor offered, "Do you need me as chaperon?"

He declined. "No, and I won't take you along for the ride either. I'm afraid it may be a ruptured duodenal, and if I have to organise hospital for this man, I don't know when I may be free. But of course I'll drop you at the bungalow first."

At parting, he kissed her cheek very lightly. "Better luck next time," he said, and was gone.

Indoors Honor debated the merits of going to bed early and of washing her hair as she had originally planned, deciding on the latter, as it would take time to dry, which meant that she would still be up to hear Dorice's account of her own evening at La Voile which she would be sure to want to give.

Honor collected the necessities of her task – brushes, shampoo, towels and a silk kimono to put on when she took off her dress, and was at the door of the bathroom when she heard a car draw up.

Now who? Adam returned for some reason? Dorice? Surely not yet. They dined late at La Voile. Whoever it was, they were inside already, just as Adam or Dorice would be. But it was Arnot, closing the door behind him as he faced her across the little hall; as she stared.

What was he doing here? Even if he wanted to see her, Dorice would surely have mentioned that she had gone to the clinic and probably somewhere later with Adam! Suddenly fearful, her voice thick, she asked, "What is it? Dorice? She – she hasn't had an accident? She is all right?"

"Dorice all right? More than – when I last saw her. She's at home," Arnot said.

"I know. She's there for the evening ... dining there. And so are you –!"

"Am I? You surprise me. I thought I was here."

"But why? What for?"

"To see you."

"But why should you expect to? Dorice must have told you I planned to be out."

"If you had been, I'd have camped on your door-step until you came back. To recap – I came to see you. *Just* you. And alone, as you may remember I've needed to before?"

"And this time – what now?" she asked wearily.

He did not reply at once. Then, his voice deepened to gravity, he said, "This time for a different reason. A – man-to-woman reason. You could say, *the* one man-to-woman reason that matters. Honor –?"

He had spoken her name on a note of question, almost of entreaty as he moved towards her, filched her prosaic armful from her and threw aside the kimono, taking both her hands into his.

At even so little intimate a touch she tensed against the knowledge of being fatally disarmed by it. He couldn't *want* to hold her hands so! But when she made to wrest them free, he held fast. She said in a small hard tone,

"I don't know what you mean by a man-to-woman reason between you and me. To you I've always been only a confederate in a plot. You said so yourself."

She saw that he remembered. He said, "On a night when I had dared to kiss you for love; wanting to explore love with you, and you had responded with about the warmth of ice. If ever I've been a clumsier fool –! I should have known that wasn't the moment – when you must have felt that by confronting Noel Bonner with a half-truth, I had forced you to touch pitch. Isn't that so?"

She shook her head. "It wasn't that. I hadn't had to lie to him. But I thought you had kissed me just because I was there – and fair game."

"Saying no to me – as I made myself say No to you when I kissed you again – in anger?"

At a new understanding in his voice she looked up shyly. "Saying no – because it wasn't possible that – from me – you could be wanting yes. As I *knew* it wasn't possible, when you did kiss me again, as if – if you almost hated me –"

"Hating your no – though still wanting you. Want you now. Shall always – But you're fortunate. A woman has only to say no; a man has to ask for his yes, and you can't know what it does to his pride to have it rejected. Then he *needs* to hurt – sometimes even the thing he loves. And some types are so fossilized by pride that they can't ask again. As I almost didn't, although I've been waiting ... waiting all these months for the chance. Honor, you're listening now. Heeding? Caring that *I* care at least? Tell me –?"

Her hands stirred in his and he released them, taking her into his arms instead.

She said softly, "I had to say no, because I thought you were in love with Ysanne."

"But you know differently now? Do you suppose I'd have let her flit off to Europe if I hadn't been almost as much her dupe as the rest of you?"

"You're going to let me leave too," she reminded him. "You've been counting the days –"

"Yes. Dreading the hour when I might have to hear your No again. But not shirking it. *Not* letting you go until – oh, Honor, if I dare hope you're really saying yes to love, need we waste any more words? Let me show you instead. Show *me* –!"

Beneath the silk of his shirt she could feel the thud of his heart matching the beat of her own as he drew her closer and kissed her with a rough hunger, asking a response which this time she did not withhold. She clung to him, feeling the hard strength of his back under her hands, and allowed her lips to flower to his, accepting and giving; their need of each other a totally shared thing at last.

When Honor turned her head, he dropped a butterfly kiss on her cheek and held her off, though not releasing her. "Do you remember," he murmured, "my promising you that the next time I kissed a woman, I'd see that she knew just what I was saying to her? Well, this *is* that next time. Have I made you understand?"

She rested her face against his shoulder. "I – think so."

"That I love you, want you, want to marry you; that I've been waiting for you, my blessed damozel, all my life?"

"Oh no." She shook her head. "That can't be true. I couldn't possibly be your – first."

"And of course you're not. You're my last and best. I realise now that in any other affair I've had I've been looking for you and, not finding you, haven't been tempted to take second-best or to snatch. I believe I even *recognised* you on the plane, coming out."

"If you did, you concealed the fact very thoroughly later," Honor said drily.

"Ah – when I judged you over Piers, and whenever I was jealous of Page whom, as he is leaving, I gather you have turned down?"

She nodded. "Some time ago."

"But he had you to himself all of every day, and you were almost always together out of duty hours!"

"Well, what did you expect? We had work in common to talk about, and he was the first man here to invite me out. He's fun, and I like him. I always shall, if we keep in touch. But between him and me the – the spark was never there."

"What spark? How do you know it wasn't?" When she did not reply Arnot prompted gently, "Because it had already lighted in you – for me? And if it had – when?"

"If I told you 'On the plane, coming out', would you believe me?" she parried.

He laughed. "There's nothing I wouldn't give to believe you, though I daren't. And anyway, even if it had, didn't our hostility bid fair to quench it later?"

"Your hostility to me, you mean?" she accused him with spirit.

Surprisingly he agreed. "Yes, I admit I engineered hostility, censure, criticism against you sometimes. While I couldn't take you in my arms and persuade you, I couldn't let you get lukewarm about our pact. Arguing to myself that in the face of the enemy one will always bare one's teeth at him and stand fast,

183

in order to show him just where he gets off. Anyone of spirit, that is, and if ever a girl has shown spirit, you –"

A little shakily Honor broke in there. "If you'd taken me in your arms and confided in me, you might have got better results and sooner. And if you weren't in love with Ysanne, why was it so important to you to keep the pact going?"

"I asked you once whether you couldn't guess why. Can't you now?" he challenged, and as she shook her head, "No? Well, primarily and as it always had been, it was to shield you from Ysanne."

"To protect *me*?"

"And to keep you here for longer than I know you'd have felt able to stay, once Ysanne had the daggers out for you."

"You mean you daren't let her know I was the girl in Australia, or she would have shown me no mercy until she did drive me out?"

"Contract or no contract with U.N.H., I was afraid she might succeed before I had held you here long enough to – let's say, to move nearer to you, my darling. You see, I did have Ysanne's measure rather better than either Dorice or my mother had, I think. I'd seen her too often in tantrums of frustration over trifles, and I'd taken the backlash of her black rage with Piers over you. It wasn't to be hoped she would give your reputation any quarter at all, once she knew who you were."

"With that snapshot of Piers, she did know who I was – or thought she did."

"Though as I told you, she wasn't quite sure enough of her facts to turn on the full heat. And at the end, she bought her passage to Europe from me at the price of continuing to hold her tongue. As you know, she pranced out, still holding it, and you were safe from her at last."

"Oh, Arnot, what a coil of intrigue, just for me!" Honor relaxed against him and he held her close again. "But Piers could have come back at any time, and where would your scheme have been then?"

"Flat on its face, I suppose," he admitted. "But it was a remote risk I judged I could run while we all thought it was he who had flung away from Ysanne, instead of the other way about. Piers Sabre, as you found to your cost, treads heedlessly on people, but he's not the type to creep to any girl."

"No," Honor agreed slowly. And then – "Do your mother and Dorice know yet about Piers and me? And about you . . . wanting me?"

He flicked the tip of her nose with a forefinger.

"Miss Need-To-Know-The-Worst!" he teased her. "Answer to both questions – yes, they know now."

"Oh –! How long have they known?"

"Just tonight, since Dorice came home."

"But don't they hate me for Piers, never want to see me again?"

"Far from it. I told you I knew what I was doing when I gave you your chance to be yourself with them, and now they both love you for it. And I have a feeling Maman didn't need telling about me and you. How do you suppose she managed to convince Ysanne that I wasn't interested in her, if –?"

"You think she had guessed?"

"She'll probably claim to you that she had sensed it

all along, bless her."

Honor breathed, "I'd give anything to believe that she is glad that it's me for you, not Ysanne."

"If she is true to her theories about marriage for love, she can't but be glad. And it never was Ysanne for me – in *this* way," he murmured against her cheek.

"Wh-which way?"

"Glutton! As if I haven't shown you already – perilously near to danger point!"

She knew what he meant – that though in their closeness there was safety for them both, there was danger too in the quickening, surging tide of their passion to which, in this first heady awareness of all they had to share, they must say no. Tonight they must stop short at promises. They had all their life together in a love-marriage for the fulfilment.

So she was content now with feather-soft kisses and his tracing of the outline of her face from temple to jawline, touching each feature in turn, as if he were limning-in a drawing that he meant to treasure. And then, an arm still about her, he was turning her towards the door. "Come along. It's time to go home," he said.

Now they were out on the dark deserted shore road, driving towards La Voile.

Honor had protested that she couldn't possibly go. "Not while you have guests. Break it to your mother and Dorice yourself, and take me to see them tomorrow," she begged.

But Arnot was firm. "Our guests will still be there tomorrow, and Dorice is staying the night."

"Oh, I didn't know that. She didn't say –"

"I think she hadn't meant to, until she got home. She'd have rung you, but now that's not necessary, and I'm not letting you out of my sight until I see you off to bed at home too."

Honor shivered with nervous excitement. "I'll need night things, then?"

"If you like, though I daresay Dorice could lend."

"And there's Adam –"

"Page? What about him at this time of night?"

She couldn't resist a little thrill at the jealous note in the sharp question. "It's only about nine o'clock," she pointed out, and explained that if Adam was free earlier than he expected, he might call in on his way to his own bungalow, and would be alarmed to find her gone. "I'll have to leave a note for him, in case," she claimed.

"All right. Do that," Arnot had conceded. But she hadn't shown him her note for Adam, which said,

"Very dear Adam – Arnot has come for me to take me home with him, and I'm going. Because – it's like a fairytale come true – he does want me, love me, as I want him. He has been jealous of you, as I was of Ysanne. But it's a lot longer story than that, though I promise you shall be the first to hear the whole of it – and from me.

"Be glad for me, Adam. Knowing you, I think you will be. Grand'terre, you, Arnot's loving me – what did I ever do to deserve it all? Arnot is waiting in the car for me, and I must go. But thanks, thanks, thanks – for everything!"

She had sealed it, left it where he couldn't miss it if he came, and went out to Arnot, who kissed her as she took her seat. "One for the road," he said, and drew away.

As if by common consent they didn't talk of the wonder that had happened for them, and Honor, for her part, was content simply to be beside him, thinking, This is what the everyday of marriage to him will be like – driving with him sometimes, not needing to talk. Or needing to, saying the most ordinary things, but with the radiance of loving him and being loved behind it all – as it would be, all her faith in him knew.

He asked her when Adam expected to leave, and she told him.

She asked him what had happened to Germain Trèves, and he said, "He didn't last more than a couple of days longer on my payroll, as you may guess, and I hear he has taken a barman's job on the waterfront. Ysanne's car was back on Pont l'Eveque on the Monday, as he had promised her. So there wasn't any charge one could get him on – he had taken it with her consent, after all."

"Though there was a charge he should have had to answer once," said Honor, deciding it was time to say so. "Of careless driving, in fact, as he admitted to me himself."

"Admitted to *you*?" Arnot's head turned sharply. "I didn't know you had ever spoken to the fellow before he shanghaied you. How? When?"

She told him about the night she had been waiting for Adam on the quays, and heard the dark menace in his voice as he said, "If I'd known that type had dared to threaten you –!" And then, musingly, "But that explains a lot. *The* lot that I didn't want to believe when I examined the damage to Ysanne's car, and knew it couldn't have been done as she claimed."

"You knew it too? So did Adam," said Honor.

"Yet neither of you mentioned it."

"Nor did you."

"No. The Ysanne syndrome at work again – shielding her at all costs. I didn't accept your idea that a man was driving and I didn't want to believe Ysanne was lying to save her own skin, though the fear that she might have done was there, and I let the whole thing drop."

"And now it doesn't matter any more."

"Nothing about that little schemer matters any more to us, my heart," Arnot agreed.

"Except –" Honor stopped, biting her lip – "your rift with Piers."

"Yes, that –" As he spoke he drew the car into the road verge, stopped and answered the question she looked at him with, "A little time gained. There's something you have to know before I take you home. Something ... some*one* you're going to have to face there –"

"Something? What? *Who?* Not – *Piers?*" she breathed.

He half-turned in his seat to clasp her hands. "Yes. Look at me while I tell you. It – helps. You see, it's he who's the 'guest' we brought Dorice home to meet. Piers and his bride of a fortnight – an orange-estate heiress, at that!"

"Piers! *Married?* Oh –!"

Arnot tilted her chin. "It's only shock, isn't it? Surprise? Just that? It doesn't hurt any more?" he asked

189

anxiously.

She laughed then, a sound of pure happiness. "Hurt? *No*. Nothing about Piers has hurt me since I came to Grand'terre. I'm just glad for him – *glad* if he's happy. But how is he here? Why? Did you try to trace him after all?"

Arnot nodded. "After the trouncing you gave me, though against my own judgment, yes. With Napier as the clue, it wasn't too difficult. It's the none-too-large wealthy centre of Enzed's citrus industry, and it seems Piers lost no time in getting next to one of the bigger estate-owners, and even closer to his extremely well-found daughter."

"She is beautiful – his wife?"

"Helen? According to Dorice, she's a honey-blonde – very cool, very poised, very sure of her appeal for Piers, and they both seem to like it that way. But she's not as lovely as *my* girl. When they made you, my darling, they threw the mould away."

Honor laughed and blushed, shy of compliments she had never expected to hear from him. "Dorice didn't know Piers had come home?" she asked.

"Not until she came over. It was Mama's idea to surprise her."

"But Piers and his wife? Isn't it going to embarrass them to meet me?"

Arnot laughed shortly. "Have you ever seen Piers lose face? He has the resilience of a yo-yo, that lad. As for Helen, I think she's already come to terms, wise girl, with his easy attraction to and for women. But he chose *her* for keeps, and that's her strong point. I daresay she'll be interested to meet one of his former flames – but she won't be wary of you, I think."

"Then *I'm* the only one to be embarrassed, and I shall be – terribly," said Honor.

Arnot started the car again before he answered. Then he asked, "Need you be – with me beside you, behind you, with you all the way? They're your family now – waiting to welcome you. What's so terrifying about that?"

Nor was there anything. At La Voile the curtains to the long drawing-room were still undrawn, and Arnot suggested they go in by the french window which gave on to the garden. He took her hand, first turning it palm upward and folding her fingers over the kiss he put there.

"For courage, and as my eternal promise to you," he whispered. Then they moved, hand in hand, out of the dark into the lighted room, and at sight of the bright, expectant faces turned their way, Honor knew she had nothing to fear.

These people, thanks to Arnot, were her people now. She had indeed come home.

Why the smile?

... because she has just received her **Free Harlequin Romance Catalogue!**

... and now she has a complete listing of the many, many Harlequin Romances still available.

... and now she can pick out titles by her favorite authors or fill in missing numbers for her library.

You too may have a **Free Harlequin Romance Catalogue** (and a smile!), simply by mailing in the coupon below.